Samuel French Acting Edition

Murder Is A Game

A Comedy Mystery in Two Acts

by Fred Carmichael

SAMUEL FRENCH

SAMUELFRENCH.COM   SAMUELFRENCH.CO.UK

MUSIC USE NOTE

Licensees are solely responsible for obtaining formal written permission from copyright owners to use copyrighted music in the performance of this play and are strongly cautioned to do so. If no such permission is obtained by the licensee, then the licensee must use only original music that the licensee owns and controls. Licensees are solely responsible and liable for all music clearances and shall indemnify the copyright owners of the play(s) and their licensing agent, Samuel French, against any costs, expenses, losses and liabilities arising from the use of music by licensees. Please contact the appropriate music licensing authority in your territory for the rights to any incidental music.

IMPORTANT BILLING AND CREDIT REQUIREMENTS

If you have obtained performance rights to this title, please refer to your licensing agreement for important billing and credit requirements.

CHARACTERS

TOBY BIGELOW
SLOAN BIGELOW
LOIS DUNSTON
JUNE RIPLEY
STEPHEN LEECH
CORA LEECH
NICK RANELLI
BB MINK

SCENE

The action of the play takes place in the living room of a hill-top mansion.

TIME

ACT I

Scene 1
Late afternoon of the present.

Scene 2
About an hour later.

ACT II

Scene 1
A short time later.

Scene 2
A few minutes later.

ACT I
Scene 1

SCENE: The action of the play takes place in the living room of a dilapidated mansion high on a hill. Since this was built for a movie set on location what is left is sparse and in very bad condition. The main entrance is through a large arch on the Up Center wall. Through this a staircase can be see leading upstairs and off L. Below this and to the L. leads to the dining room and kitchen, to the R. leads to the front door. D.R. is a large fireplace with a very carved mantelpiece, above this the wall slants up and this is a sliding panel which slides downstage. A jog is C. of this with a small table against it. The upstage wall slants up to the L. On the L. wall there is a built-in bookcase with the bottom shelf extending out to hold trays, etc. The shelves are well-stacked with old books, many of them heavy reference volumes. Below the shelves there is a pair of French windows which are open and below this a straight, wooden chair. Right C. there is a very uncomfortable and threadbare sofa with throw pillows on and to the R. there is a large, overstuffed and equally threadbare armchair with a small table to its L. A phone is on the bookshelves. The walls are bare as almost everything was removed. Perhaps they are covered in faded wallpaper or generally brown wood paneling. It is late afternoon of the present day and the sun comes in through the windows.

AT RISE: A door SLAM from off R. TOBY BIGELOW enters carrying two suitcases. He is in his forties, pleasant looking with a good sense of humor. HE is dressed casually but well. HE looks around.

TOBY. Oh, my God!

(Turns to go and bumps into SLOAN BIGELOW who is a few years younger than he is, bright and smart and beautifully and casually dressed.)

SLOAN. Where are you going?
TOBY. Home. (*Starts to go again.*)
SLOAN. No, you are not.
TOBY. Yes, I am. (*Tries to push her out ahead of him.*)
SLOAN. (*Stops him.*) You are being mean and rotten to Lois.
TOBY. But I am being kind and sensible to us. Come on.
SLOAN. (*Starts to sit in chair L.*) If you want to end a very pleasant twenty-two year marriage then go along. Until Lois shows up I am sitting here. (*Sits and leaps up again.*) Ow!
TOBY. (*Laughs and puts bags down.*) Well?
SLOAN. (*Crosses to sofa.*) Then I am sitting here. (*Sits and leaps up again.*) Then I'll stand.
TOBY. (*Moves down to her.*) The furniture had to be falling apart for the movie, remember?
SLOAN. Then where did the actors sit between takes?
TOBY. Trailers, portable dressing rooms, those canvas director's chairs, how do I know?

SLOAN. What's left here is a *House and Gardens* disaster. Did it all have to be so broken down?

TOBY. That was the story line.

SLOAN. This whole thing is a joke. Lois has left us here. It's like a snipe hunt.

TOBY. She said this was our anniversary surprise.

SLOAN. (*Looks at shelves.*) Then why aren't we at the Hilton?

TOBY. Isn't this more intriguing?

SLOAN. Intriguing, yes. Comfortable, no.

TOBY. But your favorite leading man sat in that chair.

SLOAN. He did, didn't he? (*Pats chair L. and sits again.*) It's actually quite comfy, you know.

TOBY. It is rather fun to see where that movie was shot.

SLOAN. I thought you wanted to go home.

TOBY. (*Goes to sofa.*) Remember when that pretty blonde was perched there with the storm raging—

SLOAN. The lights flickered—

TOBY. The body came tumbling through those French windows. She screamed.

SLOAN. (*Rises.*) I screamed. It was a great movie.

TOBY. (*Tests the sofa springs.*) Even renting it last night didn't quite prepare me for this.

SLOAN. *Murder is a Game.* Good title. Good film.

TOBY. Think of it. They build this old house way up on a hill-top for one movie and then abandon it.

SLOAN. (*Suddenly.*) Toby, where is it?

TOBY. Where is what?

SLOAN. (*Rises.*) The panel. The secret panel.

TOBY. That's right. It was over here somewhere.

SLOAN. (*Goes to fireplace.*) But it opened from down here.

TOBY. Maybe they did it off camera.

SLOAN. Here it is. (*Presses piece of molding on downstage side of mantel and the panel slides open.*) Voila!

TOBY. Good for you. (*Goes inside.*)

SLOAN. Any dead bodies?

TOBY. No, but here's a decent chair with a piece of paper on it. (*Comes out with canvas directors chair and a piece of script paper.*) I bet it's from Lois saying "surprise."

SLOAN. Maybe it's our royalty check.

TOBY. It's a page of dialogue from *Murder is a Game.*

SLOAN. What's it say?

TOBY. (*Reads.*) "I won't tell anyone if you'll put down that sharp dagger." Oh, great dialogue. (*Crumples paper and throws it to Sloan, opens chair and puts it downstage of fireplace.*)

SLOAN. (*Lets go of spring and panel closes.*) Sounds like your writing when I met you. There, that closes the panel.

TOBY. You were no Agatha Christie yourself.

SLOAN. (*Throws paper in fireplace and leans on mantel.*) Oh, but together—the first mystery book to hit the best-seller list for twenty-three straight weeks.

TOBY. Twenty-four but who's counting?

SLOAN. (*Straightens up.*) This fireplace is crumbling under me.

TOBY. Be careful.

SLOAN. Toby, it is paper.

TOBY. What is?

SLOAN. This fireplace. Feel it.

TOBY. (*Goes to her.*) You kid?

SLOAN. I am disillusioned. Papier maché.

TOBY. (*Pushes it in and out.*) You're right.

SLOAN. I usually am.

TOBY. What the hell did they spend their thirty million dollar budget on?

SLOAN AND TOBY. (*Nod together.*) Salaries.

SLOAN. (*Sits in director's chair DR.*) Oh, this is better. Thank you, darling.

TOBY. Any time.

SLOAN. Do you think that movie author got a percentage of the gross?

TOBY. Only after he sued.

SLOAN. We should have written movie scripts.

TOBY. (*Sits R. arm of sofa facing her.*) We did very well with books.

SLOAN. But where are we now?

TOBY. In a crumbling mansion.

SLOAN. You know what I mean. Where are we financially?

TOBY. Don't ask.

SLOAN. I just did.

TOBY. Let's say we'd better get a plot and get to our word processor.

SLOAN. Do you suppose we're the only authors with double writer's block?

TOBY. That's it. Since Lois is our publisher, she thought this setting would get our juices flowing again.

SLOAN. (*Rises.*) You really think we're abandoned here?

TOBY. No. When we started up the hill her over-priced Jaguar was in my rear view mirror.

SLOAN. Then where the devil is she?

LOIS. Here the devil is she. (*LOIS DUNSTON appears in the French windows. SHE is middle-aged or more, rather folksy but with a good business head and very pleasant. SHE carries a beautifully wrapped package, her purse and a small shopping bag with "Bigelow" books and a bottle of champagne in it.*)

TOBY. (*Rises and goes to her.*) Jaguar couldn't make the hill?

LOIS. Made it in high. I parked around the back so I could make a quick exit. Here. (*Hands him the champagne.*)

TOBY. (*Takes it.*) It's chilled. Let's open it now. (*Takes small table R. of arch and puts it L. of sofa and the bottle on it.*)

SLOAN. (*Crosses in.*) I never drink from the bottle.

TOBY. Ha! Remember on that Hovercraft from Dover?

SLOAN. It's better than Dramamine for *mal de mer.* There must be glasses in this mausoleum. Didn't they have a wrap party the last day of shooting?

LOIS. Everything you will need is here. Toby, go there to the left and into the kitchen. You'll find glasses.

TOBY. (*As HE exits through arch to L.*) And probably a passed-out character actor.

SLOAN. Lois, I have a rather ominous feeling. You said there is everything here we will need.

LOIS. (*Puts her bag by chair L.*) Correct.

SLOAN. That doesn't mean we're to say here, does it? (*Looks to LOIS who pauses.*) Does it?

LOIS. (*Nods her head.*) Uh-huh.

SLOAN. What kind of an anniversary present is this?

LOIS. Let us say unusual. (*Sits and jumps up again right away.*) Ow! This is a chair, isn't it?

SLOAN. I can't wait to try the beds.

LOIS. I admit the furniture is sparse and a bit—well—

SLOAN. Tortuous? But Toby found that chair. It's not bad.

TOBY. (*Enters with three glasses.*) It's incredible back there.

SLOAN. Three witches stirring a cauldron?

TOBY. It's all clean, neat and polished. There are glasses and plates of all shapes and sizes and I glanced in the fridge and it's full of delectables.

SLOAN. Then it's true? We are going to stay here?

TOBY. You bought this place for us?

LOIS. Wait and see.

SLOAN. (*As TOBY opens champagne at table by sofa.*) We thought we would be going from this place to some resort. We even brought evening clothes.

TOBY. Why here? Why not rent us a plot at Forest Lawn?

SLOAN. Lois, you have been a good friend as well as our publisher and—well—it isn't all going to end now, is it? Do we take you off our Christmas card list?

TOBY. (*Has poured drinks and passes them around.*) I think we need these.

SLOAN. Desperately.

TOBY. Happy anniversary, darling.

SLOAN. And to you.

LOIS. And to both of you.

(*THEY drink and SHE hands wrapped gift to SLOAN.*)

LOIS. There you are. Never in the history of publishing has there been such a gift. (*Perches on arm of chair L.*)

SLOAN. The Pulitzer. I knew it. (*Goes to sofa and unwraps present.*)

LOIS. You can't win any prize until you write another book.

TOBY. Ouch!

LOIS. You were the top mystery writing team five years in a row. You made a lot of money—

TOBY. For you, too.

LOIS. For Dunston Publishing, Inc., yes. But what happened? You rush all over the world enjoying yourselves and now you're back loaded with blank paper. Your readers have missed you. Our sales department has missed you.

SLOAN. I know. Suddenly there's nothing more to write about, no inspiration, no need. (*Tosses paper into fireplace.*)

LOIS. But there is a need, isn't there, Toby?

TOBY. Well—

LOIS. Toby has asked for an advance.

SLOAN. Money?

LOIS. That's the only advance he's tried on me.

SLOAN. Darling, why didn't you tell me we're a bit short? I'll open the safe deposit box and pawn all my jewels.

TOBY. I already have.

SLOAN. (*Shocked.*) Toby!

LOIS. And I can hardly give you an advance on nothing.

TOBY. Yes, you can. It's the present, isn't it? (*To Sloan.*) Open it quickly. It's the advance. (*Sits by her on arm of sofa C.*)

LOIS. First, another toast. To my two laziest but most favorite authors—Sloan and Toby Bigelow.

SLOAN. And to our favorite and only publisher.

(THEY drink.)

TOBY. Open the present.
SLOAN. *(As SHE opens it.)* It's smaller than a Masserati.
TOBY. It's just the size of a cashier's check. *(Deflates as SHE takes out a piece of paper.)* Oh. *(Rises.)* Lois, Lois, how sweet.
LOIS. Just what you need.
TOBY. What is it?
SLOAN. *(Kisses LOIS on the cheek.)* How sweet.
TOBY. You already said that.
SLOAN. I can't think of anything else to say.
TOBY. *(Exasperated.)* What the hell is it?
SLOAN. *(Holds paper which has the word plot written on it in large letters.)*
TOBY. "Plot."

(TOBY looks to Sloan and THEY both turn to Lois.)

LOIS. I knew you'd love it.
TOBY. Just what does it mean?
LOIS. *(Crosses to fireplace.)* It's what you need most, a plot. Once you get that, your flying fingers can speed ahead with your wry, witty way with words.
SLOAN. You mean you're actually—
TOBY. Don't interrupt. This is intriguing.
LOIS. I have rented this reconditioned-for-a-movie mansion for three days and invited some people here for a weekend of murder.

SLOAN. (*Goes below Toby to sofa.*) I adore games.

LOIS. Each of the guests has been given a character he or she is to be. They must keep to their character, assume fights and rivalries and eventually one will say, "I am dead" because the appointed murderer will have "killed" that person. You solve it and then adapt it to your own style and we have a book again.

TOBY. Have you been smoking something odd?

SLOAN. Toby, it's a great idea. (*To Lois.*) Who have you asked, Jenny and Tom? You must have put them on the list. And Millicent and—

LOIS. No one you know. That would be too easy.

TOBY. Then who?

LOIS. (*Goes to him.*) No one I know either. I handed this over to Virginia in Personnel and she said she had a ball. I am paying one thousand dollars to each of them. They each have written biographies of themselves and their relationships to each other. The weather report is for a storm which is perfect and the bridge has been repaired so have no worries.

TOBY. Worries? I am in a state of shock. (*Sinks in chair L.*)

LOIS. The beds are made, there is f   l and drink aplenty—

SLOAN. (*Rises and goes to her.*) And a caterer, please, Lois, a caterer?

LOIS. A combined butler/handyman is due at any moment.

TOBY. So we are to entertain strangers until one of them drops dead?

SLOAN. It's only pretend, Toby.

TOBY. This is one helluva anniversary present.

LOIS. I knew you'd be thrilled. (*Picks up bag with books.*) I brought some of your books to impress the guests. Where shall I put them?

TOBY. The guests are making a thousand bucks, they don't need to be impressed.

LOIS. On the shelves. (*Goes to bookshelves UL.*)

SLOAN. (*Goes to her.*) Let me help.

LOIS. There's room right here next to the reference books. Yours are just as accurate.

SLOAN. (*Takes one away leaving room for theirs.*) Get P.D. James away from us. Put her over here past *Who's Who in The East* and the AMA annual. Why did they need all these heavy books?

LOIS. The professor in the movie was always going to his bookshelves to look something up.

TOBY. He should have looked up acting. He was lousy.

LOIS. There. (*Crosses above Toby and pats his shoulder.*) I hope this game will get your atrophied brains working again.

TOBY. Something has to.

SLOAN. (*Crosses down.*) And this may be it.

LOIS. (*Starts to go, collects her bag.*) The list of guests and the rules are in there, too. (*Indicates gift box.*) So good luck and have a nice weekend.

SLOAN. You're leaving?

LOIS. (*Goes to windows.*) I'd only be in the way here and I don't want to know a thing until it's over. Besides, I have a lawyer's meeting about the partnership.

TOBY. (*Rises.*) Then the rumor is true? You're to take on Walter Matthews as a partner?

LOIS. Only forty-nine percent. It's too much for me since Gregory died. It won't change our relationship, of course. You're very special to me even if you don't get a book written. No, that's a lie. You're dirty, rotten scoundrels if you don't get a book written. Hasta luego! (*Exits.*)

SLOAN. Well!

TOBY. I don't believe it.

SLOAN. What are we going to do? Strangers are just about to burst in upon us.

TOBY. They're probably the dregs of society.

SLOAN. Let's just tip-toe out quietly.

TOBY. (*Picks up their luggage.*) We'll find a plot some place else.

SLOAN. To the car.

(*THEY start tip-toeing towards French windows but LOIS stands there holding a distributor cap in her hands.*)

LOIS. My darlings, I have to protect my investment so I removed this distributor cap from your car. Happy anniversary, again. (*Exits.*)

SLOAN. Is a distributor cap necessary for a car?

TOBY. Is vermouth necessary for a martini?

SLOAN. We can run into town.

TOBY. (*Puts luggage down by arch UC.*) You can barely jog down the lingerie aisle at Bloomingdales.

SLOAN. Then we're trapped. (*Yells after Lois.*) Just wait till you get your Christmas present.

LOIS. (*Offstage.*) Happy anniversary, darlings.

SLOAN. (*Crosses to sofa.*) Where are those rules?

TOBY. I'm in no mood to entertain.

SLOAN. (*With the rules, which are typed on paper in gift box.*) They have each been given index cards with their backgrounds and—

TOBY. —and how to interact with each other? (*Goes to her.*)

SLOAN. (*Sits on sofa.*) They better be pretty damn good actors. They have to stay in character or they lose their thousand dollars.

TOBY. What's Walter Matthews going to say about all those thousand dollar bills?

SLOAN. It could end a new partnership. And what about the IRS?

TOBY. (*Grabs rules.*) Let me see that.

SLOAN. Say "please."

TOBY. (*Sits beside her and reads.*) "Leech, Cora." That's all it says. No other hint. Oh, this is better. I know she's young and pretty and very blonde.

SLOAN. What's the name?

TOBY. "Ripley, June." So poetic. June.

SLOAN. Never trust people named for the months.

TOBY. Weren't all those "Little Women" named March?

SLOAN. Read on.

TOBY. "Ranelli, Nick." Obvious. Black hand, Mafia, Scarface, Al Cap—

SLOAN. He's probably Phi Beta Kappa from Harvard.

TOBY. The last person on the list is "Leech, Stephen."

SLOAN. That's the same as that Cora woman.

TOBY. Married?

SLOAN. Father and daughter?

TOBY. We'll have to find out.

SLOAN. They'll know from their index card bios. What else does it say?

TOBY. "Happy plotting ... Love, Lois."

(PHONE rings.)

SLOAN. *(Goes to phone.)* The phone works.

TOBY. I thought it was only a prop.

SLOAN. *(Into phone.)* Hello ...

TOBY. *(Goes UC.)* Is it Lois saying the joke's over?

SLOAN. *(Into phone.)* But you can't ... it's just not cricket ... yes, I understand but ... but ... but ...

TOBY. But what?

SLOAN. *(Hangs up.)* But we are without a butler/handyman.

TOBY. His grandmother died?

SLOAN. You guessed the usual excuse. That's Lois' way of leaving us alone.

TOBY. Anyway, now we know the butler didn't do it.

SLOAN. *(Paces below Toby.)* These people are descending on us just in time for cocktails and hors d'oeuvres.

TOBY. And who is going to make those hors d'oeuvres and dinner?

(SLOAN stops, turns and stares at him.)

TOBY. Don't look at me.

SLOAN. There is no one else here to look at.

TOBY. What dinner? Supper?

SLOAN. *(With a wicked smile.)* I have an idea.

TOBY. Ominous. It is always ominous when you use that tone.

SLOAN. None of these people know either of us, do they?

TOBY. Probably not.

SLOAN. (*Crosses to shelves.*) Except for our photos on the dust jackets of our books.

TOBY. But you insisted on all that retouching so we're barely recognizable.

SLOAN. You didn't object, Peter Pan. If these people can be someone other than who they are, why can't you?

TOBY. Why can't I what?

SLOAN. (*Hands on his shoulders.*) Be the butler-cook. That would put one over on Lois. You can sneak around and eavesdrop and solve the murder even before it happens.

TOBY. How will you explain my absence?

SLOAN. (*Moves away to windows.*) Certainly not that sick grandmother bit. I'll say my husband is off signing contracts for something or other.

TOBY. Something or other? You're such a specific author.

SLOAN. You don't look like a butler.

TOBY. Thank you.

SLOAN. But you brought your tuxedo.

TOBY. Butlers don't wear tuxedos.

SLOAN. If these people are coming here to make a thousand dollars they aren't going to worry whether a butler is correctly dressed.

TOBY. It might be fun even if there isn't a plot in it.

SLOAN. We have to do it. What choice have we?

TOBY. Now, about food and liquor?

SLOAN. Let's see how your well-stocked kitchen looks.

TOBY. (*Picks up luggage.*) First, let's take our bags upstairs and get ourselves the master bedroom.

SLOAN. Toby, dear, we cannot share the same bedroom. After all, you're of the domestic staff.

TOBY. (*As THEY exit upstairs.*) And won't that give the guests something to gossip about.

(*After a moment, JUNE RIPLEY appears tentatively around the R corner of the arch. JUNE is in her twenties and very pretty but nervous at the moment. SHE carries a small suitcase and a purse. SHE is whispering to SOMEONE behind her.*)

JUNE. I think I heard someone. Or two someones. They went upstairs. Didn't you hear them?

(*STEPHEN LEECH has entered behind her and as SHE turns downstage to look behind her, HE crosses upstage of her so SHE doesn't see him. HE also carries an overnight bag. STEPHEN is middle-aged or beyond and very much the successful businessman type and perhaps a trifle pompous. JUNE turns.*)

JUNE. Well, didn't you? (*Sees no one there.*) Oh! I don't like this. Mr. Leech, where are you?

STEPHEN. I'm right behind you.

JUNE. I thought I'd been murdered.

STEPHEN. (*Takes her bag and puts both down.*) I had to pay the cab driver.

JUNE. (*Into her purse.*) We must share that. How much was it from the station?

STEPHEN. It's part of expenses. I'll get reimbursed.

JUNE. (*Comes into the room.*) Look at this place. It scares me. This is the strangest job. Shouldn't someone be here to greet us?

STEPHEN. You'd think so unless they are playing dead.

JUNE. "They" are the authors, right?

STEPHEN. Sloan and Toby Bigelow.

JUNE. I haven't read any of their stuff.

STEPHEN. Their "stuff" as you call it is very good; sophisticated, humorous, and very clever mysteries.

JUNE. Then where are they? I want to meet them.

STEPHEN. (*Checks the bookshelves and picks up the phone.*) Hadn't we better stay in character? This room might be wired.

JUNE. Really?

STEPHEN. Why not? If we're here to give them a plot, wouldn't they want to listen in on everything we do?

JUNE. (*Takes out index card from her purse.*) My biography says you and I are supposed to be lovers. That doesn't mean that we—

STEPHEN. The operative word is "supposed."

JUNE. (*Shows him her card.*) See ... "You are the mistress of Stephen Leech" and then it goes on and on.

STEPHEN. But this is a secret liaison. (*Pulls his card from suit pocket.*) That's what my card says. It seems I have a wife somewhere, one— (*Reads.*) "Cora Leech."

JUNE. Maybe she's already here.

STEPHEN. Possibly. When I saw you studying your bio on the station platform I knew you must be one of us.

JUNE. I'll try to keep our supposed relationship a secret but I'm such a blabbermouth.

(*CORA LEECH appears in the archway. SHE is about Stephen's age, austere and lacking in humor for her role in the game. SHE wears a suit and carries a purse.*)

CORA. How do you do? The door was open and I—
JUNE. (*Intimidated at once.*) That's his fault. I didn't do it.
CORA. (*Comes down.*) So we just came in. I am Cora Leech.
JUNE. (*Points to Stephen.*) Then you are his.
CORA. Whose?
STEPHEN. (*Moves below June to Cora.*) Mine. I am your husband, Stephen.
CORA. Oh, yes, of course. Hello—er—darling. (*Offer her cheek.*)
JUNE. (*As STEPHEN pecks Cora on the cheek.*) You're very good at this.
CORA. (*Crosses to June whispering.*) Quiet! We must be who we are supposed to be.
SLOAN. I didn't see you on the train.
CORA. Bus. We were jostled on a Greyhound.
STEPHEN. We? Is someone with you?
CORA. (*With obvious distaste.*) Yes. I shared a taxi with another in our party.
STEPHEN. I'm sure they didn't want us all to meet in the city, not until we arrived here.
CORA. (*Goes to windows and glances out.*) Strange. Most strange but profitable. Now we must stay in character as we are paid to do.

(NICK RANELLI is in the archway. HE is probably in his thirties and very flashily dressed. His speech is not the best and one assumes he is not very honest. HE carries his and Cora's bags.)

NICK. Geez, this ain't no Waldorf-Astoria.

CORA. This is my taxi-mate.

NICK. I stayed in better YWCAs than this.

CORA. I believe you mean YMCA.

NICK. *(Smiles.)* Do I? Here's your bag. *(Puts both down.)*

CORA. Didn't you see that move, "Murder is a Game"? It was filmed right here. That's why the house is—well, like it is.

NICK. Yeah, swell. *(Comes down, looks at others.)* Don't stand there gawkin'. Who the hell are you?

STEPHEN. If I may be so bold, who the hell are you?

NICK. Nick Ranelli, your guest for the weekend. *(Offers hand to shake.)* Oh, you must be Toby Bigelow, this author.

STEPHEN. I am Stephen Leech. I am a former Wall Street financier temporarily at loose ends.

NICK. You kiddin' or are you actin'?

STEPHEN. I am Stephen Leech.

NICK. OK. I get it. You need the dough and a grand is a grand.

CORA. Mr. Ranelli, we are all staying in character but can't you refine yours a bit?

NICK. *(Goes to June.)* Why should I be refined when this is here for the weekend? *(Pulls index card from his pocket.)* You must be June Whatever-it-is.

JUNE. (*Moves away from him quickly to below fireplace*.) Ripley. I am June Ripley.

NICK. Yeah, so it says. Maybe we gotta get together.

STEPHEN. Not unless you are instructed to.

NICK. What's the little lady to you?

STEPHEN. Nothing.

JUNE. (*Overacting, SHE leans on mantelpiece*.) Nothing. Absolutely nothing. We do not know each other at all. We have never met until at the station today. I have never seen him before. We don't know—

STEPHEN. (*Goes above sofa, speaking to June in a whisper*.) You're overdoing it. (*To Nick*.) Mr. Ranelli, June Ripley and I are not acquainted.

(*NOTE: We must know when the guests are "acting" as they overdo it slightly not being used to performing. JUNE overdoes it the most, the OTHERS are very good at it*.)

CORA. (*Who has been looking at her index card which SHE took from her purse and now puts in her pocket, crosses C*.) Yes, Stephen, you two are acquainted and have been for some seasons past ... (*With fake tears slightly overdone*.) I suspected. Now I know. (*Goes to June*.) You are trying to steal my husband.

STEPHEN. I never saw this girl before today.

JUNE. I am not carrying on with him. (*Turns away checking her card to make sure*.)

NICK. (*Crosses down*.) Say, this is getting good.

CORA. (*To June*.) Yes, you are.

STEPHEN. No, she's not.

JUNE. No, I'm not. (*Glances at her card.*) Oh, yes I am but you don't know it.

CORA. Yes, I do.

JUNE. But it's a secret. I'm not supposed to let anyone know. Oh dear, can't we start all over?

NICK. Why? This is great.

STEPHEN. (*Dropping his character.*) You're doing very well, my dear.

CORA. Just keep at it. Follow the rules on the paper.

JUNE. I'll try. (*Back to her acting, crosses below them dramatically.*) No, no, my heart belongs to another.

STEPHEN. That's a very bad line.

NICK. You're supposed to be having an affair with me. (*Goes to her.*) Ain't that so, June Baby?

JUNE. It doesn't say so on my card.

CORA. (*Crosses C.*) Stop! Wait! Everyone be quiet. I suggest we all sit down and study our bios some more. This is getting out of hand.

NICK. Yeah, if we mess it up we won't get paid.

STEPHEN. We must stick to our parts. We mustn't stray when the Bigelows show up. (*Sits sofa R.*)

NICK. (*Glance to June as OTHERS sit.*) Maybe they ain't showin' up and we'll be able to enjoy ourselves.

CORA. Young man, sit down and study!

NICK. I just want to—

STEPHEN. Study those cards.

(*NICK sits DL and CORA on sofa C.*)

JUNE. (*Sits in chair L. and jumps up again.*) Ow!

(*NICK rises and offers her his chair and SHE sits.*)

CORA. (*Squirming around to get comfortable.*) Why couldn't they have put this film in somewhere comfortable like San Simeon?

NICK. (*Sits in director's chair.*) This chair's OK.

SLOAN. (*Comes downstairs. SHE has changed from her traveling clothes. SHE looks at them all studying, takes a deep breath and leaps into being the hostess.*) Good evening everyone.

(*ALL rise but CORA.*)

SLOAN. I am Sloan Bigelow, your hostess for the weekend. I'm sorry I wasn't down to greet you but I was unpacking. And studying. That's how I know you are Cora Leech. (*Extends hand to Cora.*) Welcome to—this place.

CORA. Thank you.

SLOAN. And your husband, Stephen?

STEPHEN. Charmed.

SLOAN. Our resident ingenue, June Ripley.

JUNE. (*Crosses in C.*) That's me.

SLOAN. (*Goes to Nick at windows.*) And Nick Ratelli.

NICK. Ranelli.

SLOAN. Sorry, Ranelli.

NICK. Your better half not here?

SLOAN. Unfortunately, my beloved husband Toby is off signing some important contracts.

NICK. That makes this weekend look even better.

SLOAN. (*Avoids him by going C as STEPHEN sits on the sofa.*) So, here we all are.

(THEY all smile at each other. A pause as NO ONE knows what to do next. JUNE sits in the chair again and jumps up with and "Ow!" SLOAN gets pillow from sofa and puts it in chair.)

SLOAN. Here, try this.

CORA. *(During above.)* We realize the movie called for this sad state of furnishings.

SLOAN. *(As JUNE sits.)* Better?

JUNE. Neat. Thanks.

SLOAN. *(Goes to fireplace.)* There may be some more chairs behind the wall. *(Presses spring and panel opens.)* Mr. Ranelli, would you mind looking in there?

JUNE. Look at that!

NICK. *(Goes into the passage.)* Geez, just like that movie.

JUNE. A sliding panel. That's eerie.

CORA. The whole film was eerie.

NICK. Here we are. What the stars use. *(Brings out a director's chair and places it C of chair L. The panel closes. HE sits in chair.)*

SLOAN. Thank you. *(Crosses C.)* Now are we all comfortable?

JUNE. *(After a pause.)* What are we supposed to do now?

STEPHEN. We were getting to know each other better.

SLOAN. Then carry on by all means.

CORA. *(Rises.)* Mrs. Bigelow.

SLOAN. Please, this must be a first name basis.

CORA. *(Goes to her, acting to the hilt.)* Sloan, I had no idea you were going to ask this—this person with us for the weekend. *(Glares at June.)*

SLOAN. Why? Do you know each other?

CORA. I know she is trying to take Stephen away from me. I wish she was dead.

SLOAN. Goody, a motive.

JUNE. It's not true. To him, I'm just another girl in the pool.

NICK. You in a bikini?

JUNE. The secretarial pool.

STEPHEN. Are you one of those typists in our office?

JUNE. (*Rises.*) Yes, sir, and you never noticed me. (*To Cora.*) Never.

SLOAN. I get the point.

CORA. She can't afford to live at the Excalibur Plaza on a typist's salary.

JUNE. (*Goes to mantelpiece and poses dramatically.*) I don't live there now. I am one of the homeless wandering from door to door.

NICK. (*Rises.*) You can wander through my door any time. (*Goes to Stephen at sofa.*) So you threw her out like a used poker hand? Men like you should be snuffed.

CORA. Snuffed?

SLOAN. That means killed. I write these things. (*To Nick as CORA sits in chair C.*) Another motive.

JUNE. I wouldn't kill a flea.

SLOAN. How about a wife?

JUNE. That's different.

SLOAN. (*Goes to her.*) If Cora Leech were out of the way, you could marry Stephen and have all the luxury you yearn for.

JUNE. Could I?

SLOAN. I stole that from an old Joan Crawford movie.

JUNE. Who is Joan Crawford?

SLOAN. I am aging right before your very eyes.

NICK. (*Sits on sofa.*) Now what? We all have motives so this could turn into a short weekend.

STEPHEN. (*Leans on mantel.*) Murder weekends don't start out this way in your books, Mrs. Bigelow—Sloan.

SLOAN. No, we always begin with a friendly—

TOBY. (*Has appeared in the arch. HE is wearing his tuxedo.*)—cocktail.

SLOAN. Precisely. (*Goes to him.*) Drinks for everyone please, Jeeves.

TOBY. Jeeves?

JUNE. I've heard that name before.

STEPHEN. (*Laughing.*) Oh, come on, whoever-you-are.

TOBY. I adopted the name of Jeeves to escape my lurid past when I went into butling. It seemed to fit.

SLOAN. (*Trying to keep a straight face.*) Thank you, Jeeves. Drinks, please.

TOBY. Will martinis suffice for everyone? That is what the Bigelows always have in their books.

STEPHEN. Perfect.

CORA. Plain seltzer for me.

JUNE. Do you have Diet Pepsi?

TOBY. I believe we do.

NICK. I'll go along with Cora but add a twist.

TOBY. You'll have to settle for a squirt of "Realemon."

NICK. You ain't got an honest-to-God lemon, just one of those squeeze things?

JUNE. It tastes almost the same. It tastes very good.

NICK. Beggars can't be choosers.

SLOAN. A martini is perfect for me as you well know.

TOBY. From your books, yes. And thank you for such a simple order. I hope you are all still here when I return. (*Exits to kitchen.*)

STEPHEN. He hopes we'll still be alive.

CORA. I'm glad a staff was provided for you, Sloan, such as it is.

SLOAN. (*Crosses and sits DL observing them all.*) It's so hard to get good help these days.

CORA. (*Anxious to get on with the plot, SHE crosses UC.*) When I was in service—

JUNE. (*Innocently.*) Which war?

CORA. Domestic service.

JUNE. (*Sits chair C.*) Oh.

CORA. When I was in service, it was an honorable calling. One was proud to be a nanny.

NICK. Nanny? What in hell is a nanny?

STEPHEN. Cora came to us as a nanny—a nursemaid and companion for my son.

JUNE. He didn't have any friends of his own? You had to hire them?

STEPHEN. Stephen Jr. was a sickly lad and needed constant watching.

JUNE. I hope he got better.

SLOAN. Oh, I think not.

CORA. After Stephen and I were married—

NICK. Wasn't there already a Mrs. Leech?

STEPHEN. She passed away.

SLOAN. (*Rises and steps in, warming up to their story.*) Soon after Cora came to work for you, right?

CORA. As a matter of fact, yes.

JUNE. How soon?

CORA.   STEPHEN.
Six months.   Nine months.

(*THEY both whip out their cards.*)

SLOAN. Well, which?

CORA. (*SHE and STEPHEN have both glanced at their cards.*) Stephen is right. Nine months.

SLOAN. (*Goes by Cora.*) And your son died soon after, Stephen?

STEPHEN. Very.

NICK. How did you know?

SLOAN. (*Goes below Cora to Nick.*) It's a well-worked plot.

SLOAN. How did he die, Mr. Leech—Stephen?

STEPHEN. Tragically.

SLOAN. (*Sits back on sofa arm.*) You turned away for a moment, didn't you, Cora, and the boy died. Was it while swimming, sitting on the edge of a cliff, bungee jumping, what?

CORA. Canoeing.

NICK. Canoeing? Come on.

CORA. (*Sweeps to windows dramatically.*) We were on a fishing trip in the wilderness. Stephen was after big mouth, wall-eyed swordfish.

STEPHEN. Salmon. We were after salmon.

CORA. (*A glance at her card.*) Yes, salmon. Fish all look alike, don't they?

JUNE. No. Salmon are pink, flounder are white, tuna are—

CORA. (*Crosses DL.*) I was just getting into the canoe when Stephen Jr. shoved off and I was left holding the paddle.

NICK. Couldn't you swim after him?

CORA. The current. The waterfall.

JUNE. This is terrible.

CORA. (*Crosses below armchair.*) I'd heard the roar of the waterfall but I thought it was from a super-highway.

SLOAN. (*Almost laughing.*) In the wilderness?

CORA. I never was very good at geography. (*Sits in chair.*)

NICK. So the wife and the son were both gone? How convenient.

SLOAN. Precisely. Then, Cora, you could marry Stephen and get all the luxury that provided.

STEPHEN. (*Steps in.*) If I thought that, I'd—I'd—

SLOAN. Kill her?

STEPHEN. (*Turns away to mantel.*) I didn't say that.

SLOAN. (*To Cora.*) And now if you are deep sixed—that's another word for killed—

CORA. Thank you.

SLOAN. —then little Miss Typing Pool here can take over. The usual plot.

JUNE. What are you saying?

SLOAN. Motives galore are abounding hereabouts.

NICK. (*Rises and crosses in.*) This chick here ain't like that. She's a sweet, misunderstood kid.

CORA. Oh, sure.

JUNE. Nick is right. I am very sweet and very misunderstood.

SLOAN. (*Goes to Stephen as NICK goes UC and glances at his card.*) Tell me, Stephen, how did your first wife die, someone leave the window open when she had pneumonia? Barbara Stanwyck was always doing that.

STEPHEN. She was shot.

CORA. Stray bullet.

STEPHEN. A hunter mistook her for a deer.

JUNE. Did she look like Bambi?

SLOAN. A hunting accident?

NICK. (*Puts his card away. Goes above sofa.*) It was a hit man. I know because I—

(*THEY all turn to look at NICK as HE stops.*)

STEPHEN. Because why?

TOBY. (*After a pause, enters with a tray of drinks.*) Happy hour!

JUNE. (*Rises, points at Toby and backs away DL.*) No, no, no!

TOBY. But it's after five o'clock.

CORA. What's the matter with her?

JUNE. He did it! Jeeves did it!

STEPHEN. Did what?

JUNE. Whatever was done. The butler did it. That's the plot they want. The butler did it!

SLOAN. Thank you, dear, but that has been done enough. Butlers are out. Start serving, Jeeves.

TOBY. Thank you, madame.

JUNE. (*As HE brings tray to her.*) It isn't you?

TOBY. Since butlers are such prime suspects, it is most difficult to secure employment. If it weren't for this peculiar weekend, I would have to seek welfare. (*Serves Cora.*)

STEPHEN. Are you pleading for a tip?

SLOAN. (*Goes C.*) No, no, no he wouldn't think of it, would you, Jeeves?

TOBY. Think of it, yes, accept it, no.

SLOAN. Very good. (*Smiles at him.*)

(*HE nods to her and takes drink to Stephen.*)

CORA. (*Rises.*) Is it possible to wash up before dinner which, I assume, will be appearing shortly?

NICK. Yeah, I could eat a horse.

TOBY. You may have to.

SLOAN. He's always joking. Now for rooming arrangements. We aren't quite sure—

CORA. (*Goes to her.*) I am quite sure. Mr. Leech and I must have separate arrangements.

STEPHEN. (*With a look to June.*) Yes, definitely.

SLOAN. (*To Cora.*) Really?

CORA. (*Whispers.*) The game. We can't sleep together.

SLOAN. Of course.

NICK. (*Crosses C.*) How about I should have a connecting room with June here to protect her?

JUNE. (*Crosses in, glances to Stephen.*) I'll have all the protection I need, thanks.

SLOAN. If you all follow me, I'll show you the rooms and you can make your own arrangements.

NICK. Cool.

SLOAN. And then we shall have dinner, shan't we, Jeeves?

TOBY. Shall we?

SLOAN. Yes. Bring your drinks along with you.

TOBY. (*Final drink to Nick.*) Your seltzer and Realemon, sir.

NICK. Thanks. I'll grab some bags and look for a john. (*Manages up the stairs with his drink and Cora's and his bags.*)

CORA. Crude person. (*Leaves her drink on the table by the chair.*)

JUNE. Don't you ever use a bathroom? Probably not. You look a bit like a camel. (*Exits upstairs.*)

CORA. (*To Stephen.*) If it is true about you and that—that typist—

STEPHEN. (*Putting his drink on the mantelpiece and gets other bags.*) A typist is as good as a nanny. You have what you want, the money, so now let me have what I want.

(*THEY are off.*)

SLOAN. Everyone has a motive for murder. They're really doing a super job.

TOBY. Bully for them. Now, what do you mean about dinner?

SLOAN. (*Trying to get upstairs.*) Lois said there was plenty of food.

TOBY. Plenty of food does not a banquet make.

SLOAN. It does if it's heated. Do what all chefs do—improvise. (*SHE is upstairs.*)

TOBY. (*Left alone.*) Four for dinner. Possible vegetarians, no cholesterol, no palm oil, and Weight Watcher's. It's going to be a Julia Child nightmare. Just call me Job. (*Exits to kitchen.*)

LOIS. (*Sneaks in windows, goes to phone and dials.*) It's me ... who do you think I mean—me! ... Yes, everything's set. There's even a storm brewing ... Yes, it's all systems go! (*Goes up to arch and looks off towards kitchen.*)

BB. (*Offstage outside windows.*) Hey, anyone in there?

(*LOIS looks for an exit, rushes to mantel and presses spring and panel opens. SHE goes into passage, panel closes and BB enters. SHE is an exotic dancer and proud of it. SHE is probably in her thirties and is extremely bubbly and intensely interested in everything. SHE is dressed flashily and has a large shoulder bag. SHE crosses C. looking around.*)

BB. No wonder they're giving me a thousand bucks. Even Oliver Twist would leave this dump. Geez, I remember that flick, *Murder is a Game*. (*Goes to panel.*) When this panel opened and— (*Goes to mantel where the spring is.*) Where was that spring? Here somewhere. That ditsy girl pushed something here.

(*SHE presses the molding and panel opens showing LOIS behind it. BB, facing downstage, doesn't see her as SHE tiptoes quickly out the windows. Panel closes.*)

BB. The hell with it. (*SHE sees the drink on the mantel and picks it up.*) A drink. Please don't let it be diet-anything. (*Is about to drink when SHE puts it down again.*) No, this is a murder weekend. I must pour my own ... (*Goes to arch and looks down where Toby has gone.*) There must be more where this came from. (*As SHE exits.*) For this gig I should have asked two grand.

JUNE. (*After a moment comes downstairs, sees she is alone and decides to practice.*) What if I'm shot? What a scene. Bang!

*(SHE practices a death scene and collapses on the sofa.
    SLOAN has come down and watches this.)*

SLOAN. (*Applauds.*) It's Oscar time.
JUNE. I was practicing in case I get murdered.
SLOAN. (*Goes above sofa to fireplace.*) You were doing beautifully.
JUNE. I've done some acting with my community theatre.
SLOAN. Neil Simon?
JUNE. We only do royalty-free plays like *Lysistrata* and *Medea.*
SLOAN. Simple costumes, too.
JUNE. Hey, I'm not allowed to talk to you out of character.
SLOAN. It will be our little secret.
JUNE. I won't be the murderer, you know. I couldn't do anything really mean, even pretend. Why in *Medea* I couldn't bring myself to kill those children so we rewrote a tiny bit.
SLOAN. (*Smiles.*) We authors should think of such things.
CORA. (*Comes downstairs in the midst of a furious but fake fight.*) No more. I've had it. It's Reno for me and, rest assured, you won't have a penny left when my lawyers get through with you.
STEPHEN. (*Following her.*) What if you don't live till Reno?

CORA. What if *you* don't? Then I'll get your life insurance and the estate.

STEPHEN. I'm changing my will on Monday.

CORA. (*Comes into room acting surprised to see others there.*) Oh, I didn't realize anyone was here. (*Moves away UL.*)

STEPHEN. Neither did I.

SLOAN. Eavesdropping is the quickest way to solve crimes.

JUNE. Even before they're committed?

SLOAN. Precisely.

NICK. (*Comes rushing downstairs.*) What's all the commotion? Someone murdered?

JUNE. The Leechs are fighting again.

NICK. (*Goes between them.*) Which one of them is going to get it?

CORA. It's none of your business.

NICK. Oh, yeah.

CORA. Unless it is your business.

NICK. What's that mean?

CORA. Stephen here doesn't have the courage to do away with me himself, but he can well afford to hire someone else to do it when he has a good alibi.

JUNE. Oh, no.

CORA. (*Goes down to her.*) And what better alibi than a witness he was with all night?

JUNE. (*Very innocent.*) Who could you mean?

SLOAN. I should be making notes. You're all so good.

CORA. (*Drops character, pleased with the compliment.*) Thank you. (*Realizes and resumes character.*) I mean, good at what?

TOBY. (*Enters.*) Dinner will be served shortly.

SLOAN. (*Amazed.*) Really?

TOBY. Campbell's cream of tomato soup is heating and, while you're enjoying that with your Stella D'Oro breadsticks, you can tell me which of the many frozen entrées you desire.

NICK. For a thousand bucks I'd lick it like a popsicle.

SLOAN. I'm sure dinner will surprise us all.

TOBY. I have an even better surprise.

SLOAN. What?

BB. (*Pops in from kitchen.*) Me.

SLOAN. You're not a cook by any chance?

BB. No way.

STEPHEN. Then who are you? You're not on my list.

CORA. (*Checks her list.*) Nor mine.

NICK. With any luck you'll be on mine before the weekend is over.

JUNE. How typical.

SLOAN. Were you invited?

BB. (*Crosses down C.*) Not by you, no.

CORA. Then what are you doing here?

SLOAN. (*Crosses to BB delighted.*) I know who you are. You're the unexpected guest. Every mystery has an unexpected guest. How do you do?

BB. (*As THEY shake hands.*) I'm fine, thanks. (*To others.*) See? She knows who I am. I'm here to join you for the weekend and be a part of—murder, isn't it? Cripes, I hope it's not me who gets iced.

SLOAN. (*Moves away R.*) Iced. What a good word.

NICK. (*Goes to BB's L.*) You won't be iced if I have anything to say about it.

STEPHEN. (*Goes to her R.*) Why are you so familiar? Have we met before?

CORA. Stephen, that is a trite line. (*To BB as SHE sits in chair L.*) Watch your step with him.

STEPHEN. Of course. You are BB Mink.

BB. (*Delighted.*) You seen my act?

NICK. I have. I just didn't recognize you with your clothes on.

CORA. And just how well do you know Miss Mink, Stephen, darling?

STEPHEN. Centerfold, calendar, nothing in person.

CORA. (*To June.*) Was Miss Mink before you, June, dear, or are you being replaced, too?

JUNE. So soon?

BB. (*Goes to Cora.*) You just watch yourself, sister.

SLOAN. Here comes another motive.

CORA. I've had enough of this. I am leaving.

SLOAN. You can't. It's not fair.

CORA. (*Goes to phone.*) I'll do as I please.

TOBY. (*Sotto voce to Sloan.*) It's part of the game. She's not going anywhere.

SLOAN. Oh, of course.

CORA. (*Jiggles phone.*) Hello ... hello ...

SLOAN. Not a dead phone. That's so usual.

CORA. No, someone's there but the static ... yes, hello, operator. I want to call a taxi to ... (*To Sloan.*) What's this mausoleum called?

TOBY. "High Winds."

CORA. Thank you, Jeeves. (*Into phone.*) It's called "High Winds" and please ... what? ...oh, no ...

SLOAN. (*Goes to sofa R.*) Here it comes.

JUNE. What?

SLOAN. (*Goes above sofa.*) Bad news always comes after all the motives are set.

CORA. (*Into phone.*) —but that can't be. The storm hasn't broken yet.

(*THUNDER.*)

TOBY. (*Crosses DR to Sloan.*) Now it has.

SLOAN. How did Lois arrange all this?

CORA. (*Into phone.*) The winds, yes. When will it be fixed?

SLOAN. The bridge. I know it's the bridge.

JUNE. The one we came over?

SLOAN. It was rebuilt for that movie.

CORA. (*To others.*) They opened it and now it won't close. Something with a computer. (*Into phone.*) When will it ... hello—hello—

SLOAN. A dead phone. That does it.

CORA. No, for real. No game. The bridge is out and the phone is dead.

SLOAN. (*Not believing her.*) Of course. Jeeves, let's eat before the electricity goes off and you can't microwave.

BB. You don't use any palm oil, do you, or—

TOBY. I use whatever is in the little microwavable dishes, ma'am. If there are any complaints, I shall leave.

STEPHEN. You can't.

NICK. None of us can.

SLOAN. And there are enough motives here to write a mini-series. Come along, everyone, let's all ride into the jaws of Weight Watchers.

STEPHEN. (*Goes UC and JUNE rises.*) Come along, Cora.

CORA. (*Shakes off his arm.*) Leave me alone.

STEPHEN. Then come along, June.

NICK. Leave her alone.

STEPHEN. Then come along, Miss Mink.

BB. Ms. if you don't mind.

STEPHEN. We can discuss it later over brandy. I never travel without my Napoleon.

BB. (*As THEY exit.*) I don't usually travel alone either.

JUNE. (*To Toby.*) Are you sure you're not going to do it? Butlers always do.

NICK. Maybe he's in disguise.

JUNE. I'm scared. The storm is brewing, the bridge won't work, and the phone is out ... (*Goes toward phone.*) Oh, why won't you work?

(PHONE rings.)

JUNE. You are working. This is eerie.

SLOAN. That's a surprise.

NICK. (*Into phone.*) Hello—

CORA. We're saved.

STEPHEN. (*Rushes back in followed by BB.*) Saved from what?

CORA. Each other.

NICK. Quite. (*Into phone.*) Here? You're sure? ... Who? ... who is this?

STEPHEN. Who?

NICK. (*Into phone.*) Hello—hello—(*Hangs up.*) It's dead again. A voice said, "There is a murderer at "High Winds."

CORA. It didn't say who?

NICK. Just "it is" and the line went dead again.

CORA. But who is it?

SLOAN. (*Sotto voce to Toby.*) Oh, please don't let one of them say, "Someone in this room."
JUNE. Then it is someone in this room.
SLOAN. I knew it!

CURTAIN

Scene 2

It is about an hour later. The room is the same except the glasses have been cleared. CHATTER can be heard from the dining room. SLOAN enters from there, glances behind her to the talk, goes to the phone and picks it up.

SLOAN. Dial tone. It does work. Part of the game. (*Hangs up.*)

(There is a KNOCKING sound. SHE looks around and sees no one. KNOCKING again.)

SLOAN. The panel. (*Presses spring on mantel. Panel opens and TOBY is there holding a cup of coffee.*)
TOBY. Does madame take sugar and cream?
SLOAN. You know perfectly well madame takes it black and what are you doing there?
TOBY. (*Comes in and panel closes.*) I saw you leave the dining room and—
SLOAN. The frozen fettucine was still cold and I wanted to check the phone. It works.

TOBY. Of course it works.

SLOAN. (*Patiently.*) I realize that now.

TOBY. (*Goes to C of sofa and SLOAN moves in and takes the cup.*) I remember in *Murder is a Game* the butler used a sliding panel in the pantry and there it was.

SLOAN. (*Sits on sofa.*) Is the passage full of cobwebs and rats?

TOBY. Only in the movie, darling. It has electricity and lots of styrofoam cups with fuzz growing.

SLOAN. Quickly, what has Jeeves found out?

TOBY. How to set a table, microwave dinners, and make instant coffee taste like perc but you'll have to decipher the dishwasher.

SLOAN. What about the plot they've hatched up? Haven't you eavesdropped?

TOBY. I've been slaving in the kitchen.

SLOAN. Lois has arranged it so everyone has something against someone but who is going to kill whom?

TOBY. After dinner, I'll take to the passages and be a voyeur. Wouldn't the *New York Inquirer* love this?

SLOAN. They're all acting terribly well, aren't they?

TOBY. But are we getting a plot?

SLOAN. Just the usual—men and mistresses, young girls and hit men, and domestics who murder everyone to marry the rich employer. Maybe after the murder—

TOBY. If we solve it.

SLOAN. (*Rises and puts cup on mantel.*) Toby, we are the Bigelows.

TOBY. We'll discuss it later. There must be a passage to your bedroom and I'll bring the leftover wine.

SLOAN. You'll sneak into my room and compromise me?

TOBY. (*Goes to her.*) With pleasure.

SLOAN. No, Jeeves, my pleasure. Always my pleasure.

(*THEY kiss as CORA comes into the arch.*)

CORA. I doubt it this is part of the game.

SLOAN. Thank you for the coffee, Jeeves.

TOBY. You're welcome, madame.

CORA. (*To Toby.*) Would it be possible for the rest of us to have coffee—just coffee without any of the additives Mrs. Bigelow seems to enjoy?

TOBY. Of course, madame.

SLOAN. Why don't we have it in here, Jeeves?

TOBY. How proper.

CORA. (*Moves UL.*) I assume this is the way all you artistic people carry on.

SLOAN. (*Moves in below sofa.*) I can't speak for the others.

TOBY. (*Calls down the passage loudly.*) People! Attention! Coffee will be served in here!

SLOAN. (*Crosses to him.*) Jeeves, I believe that is the function of the hostess.

TOBY. Sorry, madame.

SLOAN. (*Goes L of Toby and calls.*) People! Coffee will be served in here! (*Comes back into the room as TOBY exits and the CHATTER offstage continues.*)

CORA. I, of course, could mention your indiscretion to your husband should I ever meet him.

SLOAN. Are we speaking blackmail, Cora?

CORA. We are speaking survival of the fittest. (*Goes to windows.*)

STEPHEN. (*As HE enters with JUNE.*) At least the dining room had comfortable chairs.

SLOAN. (*Goes to fireplace.*) They shot an important scene in there.

STEPHEN. An interesting dinner but couldn't Lois Dunston have provided something more five-star?

JUNE. (*Goes below him to below sofa.*) I love McDonald's. They give you those cute little plastic animals when you order a Whopper and large fries.

NICK. (*As HE enters, to June.*) When we get back to town, I'll take you to a little place I know.

BB. (*Enters behind him and goes to chair L.*) I bet it's his apartment.

NICK. You win your bet. You ought to go to Vegas.

SLOAN. Let's all get comfortable and Jeeves will bring in the coffee.

CORA. (*Sits DL.*) Then what do we do, play a friendly game of Twenty Questions?

SLOAN. Friendly? There is more undercurrent here than on Hawaiian beaches.

NICK. I think someone should be feeling ill. My card says—

STEPHEN. (*Aside to him.*) Don't talk about the rules.

NICK. Sorry.

BB. (*Sits in chair L.*) What rules?

STEPHEN. Very good, my dear. You play well. (*Sits by June on sofa.*)

BB. (*Bewildered.*) Thank you.

TOBY. (*Enters with tray of coffee, demi-tasse cups, sugar, cream, and spoons and puts it on bottom bookcase *shelf.*) Coffee. It's decaffeinated so you will have a good night's sleep.

(NICK takes his coffee, hands one to BB and sits in director's chair C.)

STEPHEN. But will all of us awaken in the morning?
BB. And pleasant dreams to you, too.
CORA. By the way, Miss—what is it?
BB. Mink, like the coat.
CORA. (*TOBY hands her coffee.*) Miss Mink, how did you get here? The rest of us were given either train or bus tickets. What were you given?
BB. A train ticket but I cashed it in and hitchiked. This nice guy driving a U-Haul let me off at the bottom of the hill. I seen this house and thought I was in *Psycho* but then I remembered *Murder is a Game* and that was a comedy. (*After a pause.*) Wasn't it?
SLOAN. Unintentional perhaps.
BB. So here I am. Cheers. (*Toasts with coffee cup.*)

(TOBY gives cup to STEPHEN and JUNE refuses hers with a shake of the head.)

STEPHEN. If anyone wants a drop of brandy in their coffee, I'll be glad to go up and get my bottle.
CORA. Don't even try. It's empty.
STEPHEN. You mean you—?
CORA. I knew you had plans for that bottle and some girl this evening so it's gone.
STEPHEN. Not my Napoleon?

CORA. That was a cheap brand, hardly Napoleon but it met its Waterloo down the wash basin.

JUNE. (*Tries to change the subject.*) What about a game? Isn't that what they do on country weekends? Charades, spin the bottle, something?

SLOAN. (*Goes UC.*) What a splendid idea. Charades.

(*TOBY starts to sneak out.*)

SLOAN. No, Jeeves, you stay. (*Wickedly.*) I really want you to stay.

TOBY. Of course, if madame wishes.

SLOAN. Do you all know how to play?

CORA.	STEPHEN.	NICK.
If we must.	Naturally.	Is there a prize?

BB. We get a title and act it out, right?

SLOAN. That's it.

BB. You mean if I point to Stephen Leech you'll know the name of a play?

JUNE. Which play?

BB. *The Man Who Married a Dumb Wife.* (*Bursts into giggles.*)

CORA. (*Rises, puts her cup on table by chair and re-sits DL.*) Actually he is *Much Ado About Nothing.*

SLOAN. I think you all have the right idea.

BB. I've got a title.

SLOAN. (*Goes to her.*) All right.

(*BB whispers in Sloan's ear.*)

NICK. I hope it's x-rated.

SLOAN. Here I go. (*Holds up three fingers.*)
JUNE. Three words?
STEPHEN. (*As SLOAN nods and then points upwards.*) Heaven?

(*SLOAN shakes her head.*)

NICK. Clouds?

(*Another shake of the head.*)

JUNE. Sun?

(*SLOAN gets excited and nods but asks for more.*)

JUNE. Sun—sun—sunshade—sunshine—

(*SLOAN jumps up and down nodding.*)

JUNE. Sunshine—what else?

(*SLOAN points to Nick.*)

NICK. Macho.

(*SLOAN shakes her head.*)

NICK. But I am macho.
JUNE. No, it's male. Mailman. No, boys.

(*SLOAN nods.*)

JUNE. *The Sunshine Boys?*
SLOAN. That's it.
BB. You're very good.
TOBY. Madame is an expert.
SLOAN. Thank you, dear. (*Tries to cover slip.*) Dear Jeeves is so kind.
JUNE. I'll give one to Nick.
NICK. No, I'm rotten at games.
SLOAN. Tell Cora. She hasn't joined in.
JUNE. All right. (*Whispers in Cora's ear.*)
SLOAN. Mine was so easy.
JUNE. (*Steps back from Cora.*) There.
SLOAN. Go ahead, Cora. (*Notices CORA is not moving, her head is on her chest.*)
STEPHEN. (*Rises and goes to her.*) She's fallen asleep. How like her.
SLOAN. Mrs. Leech—
TOBY. Madame, I believe Mrs. Leech has tossed off her mortal coil.
JUNE. (*To Toby.*) I didn't do it. It was an easy charade.
STEPHEN. (*Has been taking her pulse and listening to her heart.*) Yes, my wife is dead.

(*Audible reaction from ALL.*)

SLOAN. I must say you're all acting very well.
STEPHEN. (*Crosses above chair L.*) But who did it? Why?
SLOAN. There are too many whys. Everyone has a motive.
JUNE. (*Goes to Sloan and then below sofa and sits.*) Now you're supposed to tell us who did it.

SLOAN. Give me a moment to think.

TOBY. Yes, madame, tell us.

CORA. (*After SLOAN gives Toby a glare, SHE gets up.*) Can I finish my coffee now?

JUNE. You're supposed to be dead.

CORA. (*Gets her cup.*) I've played my part so I'm not needed anymore and I would like to finish my coffee.

SLOAN. Is is fair to ask how you were killed?

CORA. The murderer—he or she—told me before dinner I was poisoned. Didn't I pick a dramatic moment to die?

SLOAN. Perfect. Now go sit over there while we solve the crime.

CORA. I might not be the only one murdered you know. (*Sits DL.*)

NICK. I suspect BB here.

BB. (*Goes over towards Cora.*) Why the hell should I bump off that old frump?

CORA. I was acting a part.

SLOAN. Now, Cora, you must keep out of this.

CORA. Sorry.

NICK. (*To BB.*) I think you're trying to take Cora's place and get the old man's money.

STEPHEN. I am not an old man.

NICK. Figure of speech.

JUNE. What about Stephen and me?

NICK. BB's got him away from you.

BB. Then how did I do it?

NICK. I haven't figured that out yet.

JUNE. You're casting suspicion away from yourself, aren't you?

NICK. I didn't have no contract on the dame.

JUNE. You're the expert, Mrs. Bigelow. It's up to you.
SLOAN. Naturally I know who did it.
JUNE. Who?
SLOAN. Don't I, Jeeves?
TOBY. Do you? So do I.
SLOAN. I knew you would.
TOBY. It is you, Stephen Leech, isn't it, Mrs. Bigelow?
STEPHEN. (*Crosses to Sloan.*) I didn't kill my wife.
SLOAN. Oh, yes, you did and very cleverly. You told us all that you had the Napoleon brandy in your room.
TOBY. You knew Cora would sample it so she could say it was a cheap brand and embarrass you.
SLOAN. So you poisoned it knowing she would throw it down the sink destroying the evidence.
BB. Geez, you two are great, but what will your husband think when you team up with the butler?
SLOAN. Jeeves is my husband, Toby. That's our trick on you and Lois Dunston.
STEPHEN. (*Goes to windows.*) Very clever and, of course, you figured it out perfectly. All we did was follow our index cards.
SLOAN. Now perhaps we can all enjoy the rest of the weekend. Since the bridge was never really out we'll go into town for a gourmet meal on us.
CORA. But the bridge is really out. That first phone call was genuine.
NICK. So was the one I answered but then it went dead.
SLOAN. The acting is over now.
NICK. (*Picks up phone.*) No, honest. (*Into phone.*) Hello—hello—(*To Sloan.*) See, it is dead.
STEPHEN. And the storm is getting worse.

SLOAN. (*Into phone.*) Hello—hello—(*Hangs up.*) You're right.

JUNE. What's that noise? There. (*Points to panel.*)

SLOAN. Toby, something's a foot.

TOBY. That's from Sherlock Holmes,

SLOAN. It's from behind the panel.

JUNE. (*As SLOAN goes below fireplace for spring.*) I'm scared.

BB. What do you think is behind it?

JUNE. Or who?

SLOAN. Here goes. (*Presses the spring, the panel opens and LOIS staggers out holding her throat.*) Lois!

TOBY. I thought you left.

LOIS. (*Staggers C.*) I—I—not supposed to—

TOBY. What's the matter?

(CORA and NICK rise.)

LOIS. (*Hanging onto Toby.*) The game—it's no game—it's—it's—

STEPHEN. (*Rushes to her.*) Get out of the way. Give her air.

TOBY. Let me see.

STEPHEN. Stand aside. I'm a doctor in real life.

JUNE. (*Rises.*) This is pretend, isn't it?

NICK. I hope so.

BB. What's she doing here?

SLOAN. Lois. Toby, what's going on?

TOBY. (*Meets Sloan above sofa.*) Damned if I know.

STEPHEN. (*Straightens up.*) She's dead. This woman is really dead.

JUNE.	BB.	NICK.
I can't even scream.	Dead?	But how?

CORA. And we're cut off from everywhere—the storm, the bridge, the phone—

JUNE. And there is no one here but us.

SLOAN and TOBY. Then it must be someone in this room.

(THEY look at each other in shock at both having said that same line.)

Curtain

ACT II

Scene 1

It is a short time later. The cups and tray have been cleared. The RAIN and WIND are heard occasionally. SLOAN is alone on stage on the phone.

SLOAN. Listen to me—I—(*Hangs up.*) Damn recording. What good is a charge card? I hope your computer breaks down.

(*Paces the room and as SHE passes windows, TOBY enters behind her so SHE doesn't see him. HE is wearing a raincoat and hat.*)

TOBY. Sloan!
SLOAN. (*Gasps and turns.*) Toby!
TOBY. Good. Characters in our books always gasp like that.
SLOAN. (*Points to phone.*) Now that phone is really sick. A recording keeps saying, "Our repair crew is working for you." And then it adds, "Have a nice day."
TOBY. That is possible but extremely doubtful.
SLOAN. What did you find out there?
TOBY. Mud. Loads of it. (*Goes into hall, to the right, to remove coat and hat.*)
SLOAN. We're really stuck?

TOBY. Like a B movie. We stay here until morning and signal for help.

SLOAN. (*Moves away C.*) How? Beat out a message on jungle drums?

TOBY. (*Comes back in.*) What do you want me to do, build a bonfire in the rain?

SLOAN. You needn't be so snippy.

TOBY. (*Goes to her.*) You look particularly lovely this evening. How's that?

SLOAN. Ah, the truth. I forgive you. (*Kisses him lightly.*)

TOBY. You are too much.

SLOAN. Now what do we do? We're in the middle of a real murder.

TOBY. Where are the others?

SLOAN. Stephen—

TOBY. Is that his real name?

SLOAN. I didn't ask yet. I'm hardly used to Stephen Leech.

TOBY. Well, he's Dr. Something-or-other.

SLOAN. He and Nick Ranelli—

(TOBY starts to speak.)

SLOAN. No, I don't know his real name either—they carried Lois upstairs. (*Goes into his arms.*) Oh, Toby, I just can't believe it. Lois murdered.

TOBY. I know, but who? Everyone liked Lois.

SLOAN. Someone didn't. Bad writing or no, it must be one of us.

TOBY. Where are the women?

SLOAN. (*Goes to fireplace.*) Cora Leech, or whoever she is, is in the kitchen with June getting more coffee to calm themselves.

TOBY. And the delightful BB?

SLOAN. Somewhere repairing herself.

TOBY. (*Goes above sofa.*) I didn't notice any imperfections.

SLOAN. She said her mascara was running like the daily double. (*Sits in chair down R.*) So what do we do, gather everyone in here and announce the murderer?

TOBY. That's Agatha Christie. Let's do it the way we do in our books.

SLOAN. But we start out knowing who the killer is.

TOBY. (*Crosses to windows.*) You do cut right to the chase, don't you?

CORA. (*Comes in from kitchen.*) It's you. I hoped Sloan wasn't talking to herself.

TOBY. Quite impassable out there.

CORA. I thought so. (*Crosses L.*) Now that I know you're not a professional cook, I take back what I said about you taking bland to a new culinary height.

TOBY. Thanks and call me Toby now.

CORA. Suddenly everyone has different names but June is still June.

SLOAN. June Ripley?

CORA. I didn't ask her last name.

JUNE. (*Comes running in worried, goes to Cora.*) You left me alone. I was talking to you and you didn't answer and I thought—

CORA. No one is going to really kill me.

JUNE. I bet that's what Mrs. Dunston thought, too.

TOBY. How's the coffee doing?

JUNE. Hiccuping. It sounds sick.

SLOAN. June, dear—I understand your name *is* June Ripley.

JUNE. (*Crosses below sofa.*) No, it's Connors. June Connors. My biography for the weekend said I could keep my first name but not the last.

CORA. And I am Cora Langmuir.

JUNE. And you're both the real Bigelows?

SLOAN. Scout's honor.

JUNE. Then you can solve the murder, can't you?

TOBY. Undoubtedly.

JUNE. Have you already?

SLOAN. Not quite.

JUNE. (*Hears KNOCKING from behind panel.*) No, no, not that panel. It's another body. Don't open it. Keep away.

CORA. (*Goes C.*) Do be quiet or I shall have to slap you.

JUNE. (*Immediate quiet.*) Do you mean that?

CORA. With all my heart. Hysteria is a lack of self-control.

TOBY. Besides whoever is knocking can't be dead.

CORA. You'd better open it.

SLOAN. It's so busy here you'd think we were giving a Tupperware party.

(*SLOAN is about to press the spring and TOBY crosses to panel.*)

TOBY. Hold it! Let's see if there is an inside handle. (*Calls.*) Hello, in there.

STEPHEN. (*Offstage.*) Hello yourself.

CORA. It's my husband, my husband who was.

TOBY. (*Calls.*) Are you all right?

STEPHEN. (*Offstage.*) Where are you, in the living room?

TOBY. (*Calls.*) Good guess.

NICK. (*Offstage.*) Can't you let us in?

SLOAN. It's Nick.

TOBY. (*Calls.*) Isn't there a way out from in there?

STEPHEN. (*Offstage.*) There's a sort of lever and— (*Panel opens.*)—and here we are.

TOBY. Bravo.

STEPHEN. (*As HE and NICK come out.*) It's like a beehive back there.

CORA. (*Sits in chair C.*) It was built for that movie.

NICK. (*His put-on tough-guy accent gone.*) I keep forgetting that.

STEPHEN. (*Goes C and NICK to above sofa.*) We put Mrs. Dunston in that small green bedroom.

JUNE. That's my room.

STEPHEN. You don't plan on going to bed, do you?

JUNE. Oh, no.

NICK. (*To himself.*) Too bad.

TOBY. While you have been wandering the walls, we have been reintroducing ourselves. June is June Connors and Cora, your wife-who-isn't, is Cora Langmuir, and you are—?

STEPHEN. Stephen Manfred, Dr. Stephen Manfred.

NICK. (*Sits on sofa.*) Nicholas Smith. I guess I can drop the tough-guy accent now, I mean, my name *is* Smith, for God's sake.

SLOAN. You convinced me you were a hit-man.

CORA. He still may be. Smith is a good alias.

NICK. What about the babe?
CORA. The what?
NICK. Sorry. I was still in character. What about the
other lady?
JUNE. BB?
STEPHEN. Where is she?
SLOAN. Oh, my God!
CORA. Not another?
SLOAN. She went to repair her mascara.
JUNE. She's dead. I know it, I just know it.
TOBY. (*Calls.*) BB! Miss Mink! Hello!
SLOAN. Hello.

(*THEY all start calling "BB," STEPHEN goes UC, TOBY
to L of arch. There is a pause as THEY all look at each
other.*)

BB. (*Enters brightly from right of arch.*) Yeah, who
calls?

(*STEPHEN crosses away L.*)

SLOAN. We thought you were—
BB. Yeah?
TOBY. Are you all right?
BB. (*Touching her hair.*) Don't I look OK?
TOBY. Dazzling.
BB. Gee, thanks.
SLOAN. We have been telling our true names and you
should, too.
BB. My real name? Oh, boy.

TOBY. (*Moves to fireplace.*) And you can drop the accent.

BB. What accent?

JUNE. Oh, brother.

TOBY. That isn't put on?

BB. Who's puttin' on what?

STEPHEN. (*As HE sits in armchair L.*) She is genuine.

CORA. And I thought you were overdoing it.

BB. Overdoing what?

NICK. Nothing, Miss—is it really Mink?

BB. Not exactly. It's Monkton, Barbara Belinda Monkton. I changed it to Monk but—(*Giggles.*) I'm hardly that so I became Mink which suits me better. Don't you think so?

STEPHEN. It is perfect.

BB. Gee, thanks. So now what happens? That corpse up there is the one who hired us so how do we get our pay?

SLOAN. I'm sure the company will t   re of it.

BB. The company?

TOBY. Dunston Publishing. Mrs. Lois Dunston, get it?

BB. (*Goes to books.*) Oh, yeah, she prints all them books you two write. She seemed a nice lady but then I only saw her dead.

SLOAN. But who hired you?

BB. I answered this ad in the personals column and was interviewed by some man. He was real cute.

NICK. He thought I was real cute but I didn't think he was real cute.

BB. (*Crosses down L.*) So that's why he didn't make a pass at me. I thought it was strange.

SLOAN. (*Crosses up C.*) Did you all answer the same ad in the personals?

JUNE. I did because I was between shows.

NICK. You're an actress?

JUNE. Trying.

BB. Gee, so am I. Do you strip?

JUNE. (*Rises and goes C.*) Oh, no. I've been in some showcases and Off-Off Broadway and I've done a lot of movies.

BB. Yeah, so have I.

CORA. I can imagine.

NICK. (*Smiles.*) So can I.

STEPHEN. What movies?

JUNE. Did you see *The Beast Who Ate Times Square?*

STEPHEN. I'm waiting till it's out on video.

JUNE. They did a close-up of me just before the beast trampled the Criterion Theatre. I screamed. I'm very good at screaming.

CORA. We know that, dear.

SLOAN. (*Sniffing.*) What's that smell?

TOBY. Something's burning.

CORA. The coffee.

JUNE. (*Screams.*) I forgot. (*Starts to run out, turns.*) I screamed again, didn't I?

CORA. Yes, dear.

TOBY. I'll come with you.

JUNE. Thanks. We shouldn't be alone. (*Exits kitchen.*)

TOBY. I think I'll still be alone. (*Follows her off.*)

SLOAN. (*Goes to Cora.*) You all know who Toby and I are so let's get on with you, Cora.

CORA. I work for the Trendy Travel Agency. I've booked all sorts of mystery trips: overnights, weekends, even one on the QE2.

SLOAN. A murder cruise?

CORA. That's it. When I saw this ad in the personals saying to make money on a mystery weekend, I couldn't refuse. Besides it's my job to check out all sorts of trips so I'm drawing double pay.

BB. You hit the jackpot. I don't have another gig for a month and so I applied and when they told me it was in the country, I got real excited. I was brought up on a farm.

NICK. An authentic farmer's daughter. I could have guessed.

JUNE. (*Returns with TOBY behind her carrying tray with coffees poured and creamer and sugar. JUNE goes to fireplace.*) Are we all still here?

TOBY. And alive?

SLOAN. At latest count.

TOBY. Since I am no longer Jeeves you can help yourselves to Cremora and Equal. (*Puts tray on table center of sofa.*)

SLOAN. Toby, we're having Show and Tell. Dr. Manfred, you're next.

STEPHEN. My relaxation from practice has always been mystery stories. My receptionist at the office said she was going to apply for this weekend. I couldn't resist. I got it. She didn't. I'm looking for a new receptionist.

SLOAN. Nick?

NICK. (*Rises.*) I'm in the hotel business, a Cornell graduate in fact.

TOBY. Where are you now?

NICK. On two weeks vacation. I'm assistant manager at the Desert Dunes, that hotel on the Vegas strip.

BB. I played there.

NICK. (*Goes to BB at windows.*) When I said you were familiar it wasn't just as Nick Ranelli. I honestly did think so.

BB. And we meet over a dead body. Gee, ain't life an endless bunch of surprises.

CORA. You could put it that way.

SLOAN. This has all been very interesting except for one thing.

STEPHEN. Which is?

SLOAN. Someone is lying.

TOBY. We are the only two here who seem to have some connection to Lois Dunston and we didn't kill her, so—

JUNE. You mean one of us—?

SLOAN. Oh, do stop saying that. Of course it is one of us.

JUNE. But which one?

SLOAN. Quiet!

BB. (*Gets coffee from table C.*) It's not me. I'm no good at lying.

STEPHEN. How do we know you are who you say you are?

BB. Well, what about you, Dr. Whatever? Anyone can say he's a doctor. I could say I'm Madame Curry.

SLOAN. Curie. Madame Curie.

BB. (*Crosses and sits down L.*) Whatever.

TOBY. This is getting us nowhere.

NICK. (*Goes to Toby.*) I'm going to skip the coffee and have one of those wonderful seltzer and Realemons you mixed so beautifully.

TOBY. I worked my way through Princeton as a bartender.

SLOAN. (*As TOBY starts to exit.*) Don't you dare.

TOBY. Dare what?

SLOAN. Get him his seltzer and Realemon. You're not Jeeves anymore.

TOBY. No, but I am the host.

NICK. Sloan is right. We should all fend for ourselves. Anyone else for a soft drink?

SLOAN. Or a hard one? I'd offer to be the designated driver if anyone had a car that worked.

JUNE. (*Sits on sofa.*) I'll have one of your drinks, Nick. It sounds refreshing.

NICK. Anyone else?

BB. I'll stick with coffee. I don't want to fall asleep. I mean, y'know, it might be the big sleep.

CORA. I am only drinking what a lot of you have tasted first.

STEPHEN. Very clever, Cora.

NICK. (*As HE exits.*) Have it your own way.

STEPHEN. (*Gets coffee and sits on sofa.*) Why should there be another murder?

TOBY. None of you apparently has any connection with Lois yet there is a motive somewhere.

SLOAN. But whoever did it wouldn't have a reason to strike again, would he? (*Pause.*) All right, don't answer me.

TOBY. Some one of us must be here under false pretenses. Look what we have: a doctor and what do we know about him? Maybe he was drunk while operating on someone.

STEPHEN. (*Laughs it off.*) I never drink before operating.

CORA. The patient died and it was Lois' brother.

BB. (*Caught up in the act.*) No, no, her lover.

CORA. All right, her lover.

JUNE. (*Adding to the story.*) And Lois found out from a nurse and she was going to prosecute Stephen so he killed her.

STEPHEN. Now, wait a minute.

SLOAN. (*Crosses UC.*) But that nurse is now blackmailing him and so he has to get rid of her, too.

BB. The poor kid.

CORA. But would he know what she looked like under her operating room mask?

TOBY. Her perfume?

SLOAN. He sniffed it here tonight.

BB. Not me. I'm no nurse.

JUNE. (*Rises and goes C acting her heart out.*) It's me. I did it! I blackmailed him. I am guilty of whatever it is. (*Faints to the floor.*)

BB. Y'know, she's really good.

NICK. (*Comes in with the two drinks.*) June, what are you doing?

JUNE. (*Sits up.*) I'm acting.

BB. It's time for an Emmy.

STEPHEN. You had me worried.

SLOAN. We were just supposing who could be guilty.

JUNE. (*Rises and goes below chair L.*) And I got carried away. It was an improv.

CORA. A what?

BB. That means she just makes it up as she goes along.

JUNE. I heard a good cue so I just went with it.

NICK. You better drink this. (*Hands her the drink from above the chair.*)

JUNE. Thanks. (*SHE sits.*)

STEPHEN. You almost convinced me I was a murderer.

SLOAN. You see, it could be anyone. Cora, here, could be embezzling from the travel agency that plans authors' book tours and Lois was going to expose her.

CORA. And June could easily be a home-wrecker.

BB. Or me. I could wreck a home again. I done it before.

NICK. (*Goes to mantel.*) Perhaps the Bigelows aren't the Bigelows. How do we know?

STEPHEN. (*Rises and goes UC.*) Yes, perhaps you are not who you are. (*Puts his arm over titles to their books.*) If you're the authors then tell me the names of these books you wrote.

SLOAN. Of course. There's—well—Toby, you tell him.

TOBY. (*Moves in behind Sloan.*) *The Maudlin Maniac, Race For Death, The—*

SLOAN. *Spy Who Came in From the Cold.*

TOBY. No, dear, that was Le Carré.

SLOAN. I always liked that title. And we wrote *Murder Comes A'courting,* and *Murder For Mischief* and—

STEPHEN. That's enough.

NICK. (*Having taken a slip of his drink.*) June, don't drink that.

JUNE. Why not?

NICK. Mine tastes funny.

BB. Oh-oh.

SLOAN. Does it smell of bitter almonds.

NICK.   JUNE. (*Smells her*
No.   *drink.*) Not mine.

TOBY. That's cyanide. He'd be dead by now.

CORA. Can we analyze it somehow?

STEPHEN. (*Crosses in above chair.*) I don't have my doctor's bag with me.

SLOAN. Do you feel all right?

NICK. (*Crosses in below sofa.*) So far, I'm—oh, my God! Look! (*HE points towards bookcase.*)

TOBY.   BB.   CORA.
What?   At what?   Where?

NICK. (*Moves in UC.*) It's—it's—don't you see? There! Now we know who the murderer is.

SLOAN. We do?

TOBY. Good for us.

NICK. The mistake. There's the one misstep.

CORA. (*Rises.*) What is the clue?

STEPHEN. And who is it?

NICK. Can't you see?

SLOAN. See what?

(*THEY all look towards the shelves.*)

NICK. Obviously, it's—yes—I do feel strange.

STEPHEN. (*The doctor rushing to his patient.*) Let me help you. Don't talk.

SLOAN. (*By his right, puts his drink on the table.*) Yes, do talk.

TOBY. What's the clue? What did you see?

NICK. I—my mouth—paralyzed—I—(*HE can't talk.*)

JUNE. Nick, Nick. (*Puts her finger in her drink and tastes it.*)

BB. (*Rises.*)   CORA.
What'll we do?   Brandy, coffee, something.

SLOAN. Who did it?

TOBY. (*Looking toward bookshelves.*) What is the clue over there?

STEPHEN. This man can't talk.

(*NICK collapses against Stephen.*)

JUNE. My drink, too. Poison!
CORA. But who did it?
BB. Then it must be—(*Looks at others.*)
TOBY. Yes, it must be one of us.
SLOAN. (*Shocked.*) Toby! You said it, too!
TOBY. (*Sheepishly.*) I guess people really do say that line.

Curtain

Scene 2

A few minutes later. SLOAN is on the phone very agitated.

SLOAN. Damn. (*SHE hangs up and TOBY enters from the kitchen carrying a Realemon.*)

TOBY. Every time I come into this room you are on that phone saying "damn."

SLOAN. That's because every time you come into this room there is a dead body being carried upstairs.

TOBY. Are we sure Nick is dead?

SLOAN. No one is going to put whatever-it-was into that Realemon thing and then not silence him for good.

TOBY. (*Holds up Realemon.*) You're right.

SLOAN. Of course I am right.

TOBY. You're also rather irritating.

SLOAN. Perhaps if I were wrong once in awhile it would relieve the boredom.

TOBY. I'll go out and come in again. (*Starts to exit.*)

SLOAN. Toby don't. (*Goes to windows.*) I'm sorry but I'm all at sixes and nines.

TOBY. It's sixes and sevens.

SLOAN. You see, I don't even know where I am. (*Sinks onto chair down R.*) Oh, Toby, why did Lois ever start this?

TOBY. (*Crosses down.*) To give us a plot.

SLOAN. She should know you can't give authors plots especially without an ending.

TOBY. (*Sits in chair.*) And the beginning is pretty lousy, too.

SLOAN. But we have all the trappings of a classic: the storm, the cast isolated, the phone and the bridge both out, and two murders.

TOBY. Readers expect at least two.

SLOAN. Poor Nick. I rather liked him.

TOBY. He was certainly better as himself than acting that hit man.

SLOAN. If he was acting.

TOBY. They're all acting but one of them is a real murderer.

SLOAN. (*Goes to him.*) We ought to be able to solve this. It's nowhere near as good as we write. (*Sits on the arm of his chair.*) Let's start again. We have Cora Langmuir, June Connors, Nick—what's his last name again?

TOBY. Smith. Do you believe it?

SLOAN. Yes. There have to be a few legitimate Smiths. We have Dr. Stephen Manfred, BB Mink—

TOBY. And two bodies at last count.

CORA. (*Appears coming down the stairs.*) One body.

TOBY. Lois and Nick.

SLOAN. (*Rises.*) If one body has disappeared then we've solved it. (*Goes below sofa.*) The first one killed isn't really dead and turns out to be the murderer. It's stolen from Agatha Christie and—

CORA. (*Crosses down.*) Stop chattering.

SLOAN. I am not chattering.

TOBY. (*Rises.*) Perhaps babbling is the kinder word.

SLOAN. But one corpse is gone.

CORA. I am trying to tell you there is only one. Nicholas Smith is not dead.

SLOAN. Yet. You're going to add "yet," aren't you?

CORA. All right, "yet." Are you satisfied?

SLOAN. Did he say what he was pointing at over there?

TOBY. He can't speak, can he?

CORA. Not—

SLOAN. Yet?

CORA. (*Nods.*) Yet.

TOBY. (*As SLOAN sits on sofa.*) It's not cricket if he gets poisoned and collapses, revives, and then says who the murderer is.

CORA. He is hanging onto life—

SLOAN. —by a thread, right?

CORA. (*Sits by her.*) Why am I telling you all this if you know it already?

SLOAN. If you start us off with a familiar speech we can finish it, can't we, Toby?

TOBY. Unless you say, "The murderer is—" and then we're stuck.

CORA. If Nicholas awakens he will tell us. (*Points to Realemon in Toby's hand.*) That's the culprit, isn't it?

TOBY. (*Puts it on table by sofa.*) It must be. The murderer knew Nick would squirt this into a seltzer sooner or later.

SLOAN. But June had the same drink, too.

TOBY. It wasn't what she ordered earlier, was it? The murderer didn't mean to kill June.

CORA. He must have no conscience.

SLOAN. You're right.

CORA. Whatever Nicholas was pointing at must have incriminated the killer but the poison was   ready in his drink before he pointed.

TOBY. (*Goes to fireplace.*) So he was being murdered before he knew who the killer was.

SLOAN. Doesn't make sense. I demand plots make sense.

TOBY. Might I remind you of *The Corpse With the Sleepy Eye*?

SLOAN. Not that again?

TOBY. You thought up the slingshot through the French doors.

SLOAN. A clever first draft.

TOBY. Not when the doors were closed.

SLOAN. You didn't catch it till the final rewrite.

CORA. If you two will stop bickering—

SLOAN. We are not bickering. We are discussing.

TOBY. You should be around when we're writing.

CORA. (*Picks up Realemon.*) The big question is why the poison was put into Nick's drink and when it was.

SLOAN. (*Rises and goes C.*) Perhaps Nick wasn't telling us who the murderer was. Perhaps they were in partnership and he suddenly noticed the fatal slip.

TOBY. We authors always say that, "the fatal slip."

SLOAN. (*Crosses towards shelves.*) And that's what he was pointing at.

CORA. "The fatal slip." That's very good. Are your books really that clever?

TOBY. Even more so.

CORA. Then I must get to a library.

SLOAN. Wouldn't you rather get to a book store and buy them?

CORA. Why buy when you can rent?

SLOAN. I've never been able to answer that to my advantage.

BB. (*Comes downstairs helping a weeping JUNE.*) I'm sure he's going to be all OK. You'll see.

JUNE. I'm not so sure. Dr. Leech—

CORA. Wrong name. He's not my husband.

JUNE. I keep forgetting who everyone is. But that Doctor—

BB. Manfred.

JUNE. Dr. Manfred said Nick might not—might not— (*SHE is wailing.*)

BB. (*Goes above sofa.*) Does anyone have smelling salts? Isn't that the thing for hysteria?

CORA. Either that or a slap across the face.

JUNE. No. I'm anti-violence.

SLOAN. Sit down over here, dear. (*In chair L.*) We're all anxious about Nick and there's nothing we can do but wait.

CORA. Together. If we are all together then the guilty one can't strike again.

JUNE. Why should anyone else get killed?

TOBY. (*Moves C.*) If Nick is in cahoots with the murderer—

JUNE. What are you saying?

TOBY. (*Speaks louder.*) If Nick is in cahoots—

JUNE. I heard you.

SLOAN. I love that word "cahoots." We should use it more often.

BB. (*Goes to fireplace.*) You think Nick might be in partnership with someone?

CORA. If he is, then it's—

SLOAN. I know, "someone in this room."

TOBY. (*Nods.*) Yes, "one of us"—

SLOAN. "But which one?" (*Sighs and sits in director's chair C.*) There, we have those lines out of the way again.

BB. Are you going to make this a book?

SLOAN. If the ending is good enough.

BB. I read one of your books once.

TOBY. (*With a glance to Cora.*) From the lending library? (*Goes to windows.*)

BB. Someone left it on the subway.

SLOAN. Did you enjoy it?

CORA. I bet there weren't enough pictures.

BB. I liked it. If you write this up it will become a mini-series and perhaps I can play you.

SLOAN. Why, how flattering.

BB. I think my future is in character roles.

TOBY. Don't you think Sloan could play herself?

BB. She's not the type. Remember that movie when Sigourney Weaver plays that dame protecting the gorillas?

CORA. You are referring to Dian Fosey.

JUNE. I saw that movie, too.

BB. Well, Sigourney Weaver got that part because Ms. Fosey wasn't the type.

CORA. Also she was dead.

BB. Yeah, but after this weekend Mrs. Bigelow might be dead.

TOBY. Or you might be dead, too.

BB. Geez. We better catch the murderer. (*Sits chair R.*)

SLOAN. Somehow one of you had a motive to kill Lois or was paid to—what did you say, BB—ice her?

BB. Yeah, that's the word of the mouth.

TOBY. But which of you is it?

CORA. I didn't even meet Mrs. Dunston.

JUNE. Me either.

SLOAN. (*Rises and goes to above June in chair.*) How do we know? You might be her illegitimate daughter and you've never forgiven her for giving you up for adoption.

TOBY. And now you want her estate.

JUNE. My birth certificate's in my purse. You want to see it?

SLOAN. (*Goes to Toby.*) It was just a shot in the dark.

TOBY. That's a good title.

SLOAN. It's been used.

BB. (*Crosses C.*) I didn't know Mrs. Dunston either. I am innocent.

TOBY. Ha!

BB. I mean innocent of the murder.

SLOAN. (*Goes to BB.*) You could be the mistress of Walter Matthews.

BB. Who?

SLOAN. Walter Matthews, the millionaire who is going into partnership with Lois.

BB. And he is throwing me over for this Lois and so I ice her? Yeah, I could play that part perfect. (*Moves above sofa.*)

CORA. I think we can safely say that none of us is the murderer.

SLOAN. But it must be one of us. (*Moves above chair C.*) There, now you've got me saying that stupid line.

TOBY. Maybe one of us but not necessarily in this room.

CORA. Why not?

SLOAN. Because we're not all here.

STEPHEN. (*Enters from upstairs.*) Now we are.

BB. (*Moves to fireplace.*) I forgot about you.

STEPHEN. I'm immune to flattery. Am I being accused of something?

TOBY. We're just saying that any of us could be the killer.

STEPHEN. You're right, of course. I could have been drunk when I operated and killed someone. How about Mrs. Dunston's daughter?

JUNE. That's me.

STEPHEN. What?

JUNE. Before, when they said I could be guilty, I was her daughter.

TOBY. But Lois didn't have a daughter.

STEPHEN. Lucky for me.

BB. Unlucky for the daughter.

JUNE. But then I'd be dead.

BB. (*Sits by Cora on sofa.*) You poor kid, so young, too.

CORA. Perhaps this is the perfect crime.

BB. I thought that was impossible.

TOBY. It is.

BB. Then why don't you solve it?

SLOAN. We do have a clue but it's upstairs inside Nick and he can't speak. (*Goes to Stephen.*) Stephen—Doctor—what is the prognosis?

BB. Prognosis? What a good word. So professional.

SLOAN. Thank you.

BB. What's it mean?

STEPHEN. The outcome.

JUNE. And what is his outcome?

STEPHEN. Nicholas was most definitely poisoned.

TOBY. (*Crosses down.*) We know that. From the Realemon.

STEPHEN. I am positive it is a poison called Digitaphallanx.

CORA.	JUNE.	BB.
What is that?	Oh, no!	I am completely lost.

TOBY. Again, please.

STEPHEN. Digitaphallanx.

SLOAN. (*Crosses below him and sits in director's chair.*) South Africa. These poisons always come from South Africa. Also effective in blowguns.

STEPHEN. Correct, except it's from South America.

TOBY. Are you sure that's what it is?

STEPHEN. I've had two patients with these same symptoms and both of them had been up the Amazon.

SLOAN. Scientists beating through the brush with machetes?

STEPHEN. No, butterfly collectors. There is a plant there called Digitaphallanx by scientists and something like Willonka by the natives.

CORA. How do you know so much about this?

STEPHEN. I specialized in tropical diseases after med school.

JUNE. Will Nick recover?

STEPHEN. It's hard to say. (*Goes below sofa to mantelpiece.*) There's nothing to do now but wait for the crisis to pass.

SLOAN. Near dawn. Crises are always near dawn.

CORA. In the meantime we're the suspects so someone question us.

SLOAN. We're in the living room like suspects are supposed to be. Toby, ask something.

TOBY. (*Turns away to windows.*) What am I supposed to do, say "Everyone who is innocent raise your hand"? (*Turns back into room to see ALL HANDS raised except BB's.*)

SLOAN. BB?

BB. Oh, me. too. (*Raises her hand.*)

SLOAN. Someone is lying. (*Quickly to others.*) And don't anyone dare say, "but which one?"

CORA. Shouldn't we start with Nicholas pointing over there? Was he indicating a cohort as we suspected or was he pointing to a clue?

SLOAN. (*Goes above chair.*) There is nothing there but shelves of books including our very clever ones right— (*Stops as SHE sees something.*)

TOBY. What is it?

SLOAN. (*Points to books.*) Look!

TOBY. Where?

SLOAN. There.

(*TOBY goes to shelves.*)

JUNE. (*Rises and goes UC.*) There's nothing there but an empty space.

SLOAN. That's just the point.

TOBY. Sloan, you are marvelous.

SLOAN. We think as one, don't we, darling?

TOBY. Precisely.

CORA. What are you talking about ?

BB. Why is an empty space so important?

JUNE. (*Sits in director's chair C.*) Oh, be quiet and listen.

STEPHEN. You mean nothing being there is a clue?

TOBY. (*Goes below Sloan to C.*) Yes because something was there earlier. Tell him, Sloan, tell him what is missing?

SLOAN. I don't know. I thought you did.

TOBY. Lois put ours there among the reference books because she joked about ours being just as accurate.

CORA. Then it's a reference book that's missing?

SLOAN. And it wasn't earlier this evening. The title was—was—

(SLOAN and TOBY stand looking at the shelves.)

CORA. Dictionary, Thesaurus, Columbia Encyclopedia—?

JUNE. *Book of Knowledge?*

BB. *Lady Chatterly's Lover?*

JUNE. That's not a reference book.

BB. It was for me.

CORA. *Who's Who?*

SLOAN. That's it.

TOBY. Why *Who's Who?*

SLOAN. Not quite a *Who's Who* but the medical directory for the east. It was a who's who of doctors so why would that be gone?

BB. Who cares about a lot of doctors?

TOBY. Only someone who is *not* listed.

SLOAN. I'll wager my next royalty there is no Stephen Manfred.

STEPHEN. Are you saying I am not a doctor?

SLOAN. You took that book so we wouldn't be able to verify your story.

STEPHEN. Why should I want to kill Mrs. Dunston?

BB. Sex.

CORA. What?

BB. Sex always comes into it.

JUNE. No, love. She thwarted you, didn't she?

STEPHEN. I didn't even know her.

CORA. Power. It has to be for power. Lois Dunston was a very important and powerful publisher.

STEPHEN. She wasn't that powerful. She'd already signed away forty-nine percent of the company.

TOBY. How did you know that?

STEPHEN. Newspapers, the *Wall Street Journal*.

TOBY. Lois said it was a secret and no one knew.

STEPHEN. Leaked to the press. There's always a stoolie in an office.

CORA. I think you did know Lois Dunston.

SLOAN. (*Suddenly SHE points at Stephen too excited to speak.*) Ah—as—ah—ah—

TOBY. What does all that mean?

SLOAN. Of course. I've got it!

JUNE. I'm glad somebody knows.

SLOAN. (*Rushing through titles of books.*) Thank God for reference books.

BB. I should read more. Do libraries take Diner's Club?

JUNE. No, but they have take-out.

BB. I thought that was only Chinese libraries.

(*THEY look at her.*)

BB. That was a joke.

SLOAN. (*Pulls book from shelves.*) Here it is.

CORA. (*Rises and goes C.*) Which one is it?

TOBY. *Publisher's Annual.*

STEPHEN. That won't prove anything.

SLOAN. (*As SHE looks for the correct page.*) I think it will. Here it is. I knew I'd seen this photograph before.

STEPHEN. (*Moves above sofa.*) So you found a photo of Lois. So what?

TOBY. (*After SLOAN points to it.*) That's it! Darling, you are the better half of this writing team.

SLOAN. We agree on that.

CORA. What did you find?

SLOAN. (*Shows her the book.*) There! (*Hands book to TOBY and gets another.*)

CORA. The awards banquet? That table of people?

TOBY. (*Looks closely.*) That is Lois Dunston.

STEPHEN. Come on, what have you found?

JUNE. (*SHE and BB rush over.*) But that's—

TOBY. Yes, it is.

BB. Hey, that's a Chanel suit Mrs. Dunston is wearing. I got an exact copy at Filene's basement.

TOBY. (*Goes to Stephen.*) What have you to say for yourself?

STEPHEN. Nothing till I know what you're going on about.

CORA. That is you sitting with Lois.

JUNE. Definitely you.

SLOAN. Now look at this one.

BB. What book is it?

STEPHEN. Yes, what?

SLOAN. *Moguls, Business Giants of the 80's.*

JUNE. Who is in that?

BB. Not me. I am not a mogul. I think I'm not.

SLOAN. (*Looks at Stephen after showing book to Toby.*) I guess that does it.

STEPHEN. Does what?

TOBY. (*Goes below others to Stephen.*) You can drop the doctor bit.

SLOAN. Walter Matthews.

CORA. You're THE Walter Matthews?

BB. First he's not Stephen Leech—

JUNE. Then he's not Dr. Manfred.

CORA. THE Walter Matthews?

STEPHEN. (*To Sloan.*) It was my saying Lois signed away forty-nine percent, wasn't it?

SLOAN. You slipped up there.

JUNE. The fatal slip like you said.

TOBY. You weren't content with forty-nine percent of the Dunston Publishing empire. By getting Lois out of the way you'd get full control as you wanted.

STEPHEN. (*Crosses to fireplace.*) Wanted? I needed it. I'm only rich on paper. I couldn't even buy lunch without my American Express card.

BB. I never leave home without it either.

SLOAN. So you arranged this whole weekend?

STEPHEN. Lois told me about her plans and I said I would organize it for her. I thought I could use the game as a cover-up.

TOBY. And poor Nick was in it with you?

STEPHEN. You're wrong there. He was pointing at the empty space where the reference book had been. He'd figured it out.

SLOAN. Before us?

TOBY. That's ego-busting.

BB. (*Goes to phone.*) Shouldn't we call 911?

STEPHEN. (*Crosses below sofa.*) And send me to jail? No way. Give me that. (*Grabs Realemon from table and squirts some in his mouth.*)

BB.	JUNE.	CORA.
He's thirsty.	Stop him!	The easy way
		out.

SLOAN. No, don't!

TOBY. You think that wraps it up nicely?

STEPHEN. It's over for me. No more murders. You're a damn clever couple. (*Collapses and dies on sofa.*)

(*BB goes down L.*)

CORA. Stephen—
JUNE. The same poison he gave Nick.
BB. Is he dead?

(*CORA sits in chair L. and BB sits down L.*)

CORA. He soon will be.
JUNE. (*Sits in chair C.*) I don't believe it.
TOBY. (*Goes down by the sofa. Calmly.*) Neither do we.
SLOAN. (*Goes to right of sofa.*) Not a bit of it. We are in tune, aren't we, Toby?
TOBY. Exactly.
CORA. What are you talking about?
TOBY. You can get up now, Walter Matthews.
BB. He can't get up. He's dying.
SLOAN. (*Laughs.*) Come now. Digitaphallanx? Really.
TOBY. We know every poison in every foreign jungle. They've all been used.
SLOAN. And you were the only one who pronounced Lois dead.
TOBY. And you knew about the contracts being signed.
SLOAN. And you're not destitute. Far from it. According to that book you're among the top twenty most successful.
CORA. Is all this true?
SLOAN. (*Leaning over him.*) Is it, Walter?

STEPHEN. (*Opens his eyes and sits up.*) Yes.

BB. He ain't dead!

JUNE. What is going on?

STEPHEN. (*Gets up and goes C.*) Well, it was a good anniversary present, wasn't it?

TOBY. (*Laughs.*) The best.

SLOAN. (*Has gone and indicates for Toby to press spring.*) Toby.

TOBY. You're right. Here's another present.

(*TOBY presses spring, panel opens and LOIS is there with her ear to the wall eavesdropping.*)

SLOAN. I knew it!

BB. (*Rises.*)	JUNE. (*Rises.*)	CORA.
Who's she?	You're still here?	Eavesdropping.

LOIS. (*Crosses to Sloan at C.*) You did it! You two did it! Congratulations.

SLOAN. (*Kisses her.*) Thank you, darling. It was wonderful.

TOBY. Except for the food.

SLOAN. (*To the others.*) You all had to be in on it, didn't you? It couldn't have worked unless you all knew it was a hoax. You not only acted before Lois' death but afterwards, too.

TOBY. Two sets of characters. You're better than the Moscow Art Theatre.

LOIS. I told you the Bigelows were clever. It's over everyone. You were terrific.

STEPHEN. (*Goes to Lois.*) And we'll publish anything you write.

LOIS. And my fifty-one percent agrees.

SLOAN. Now for a moment of truth. (*To Cora.*) You must be—what?—Walter's executive secretary.

CORA. (*Meets Stephen at C.*) Hardly. I am his wife.

SLOAN. Well, I am glad to meet you.

BB. They're married?

CORA. Yes, BB.

BB. (*Sits DL watching interestedly.*) This is so exciting.

SLOAN. And you are—?

JUNE. June Matthews, daughter to those two nice people.

TOBY. It's a family reunion.

LOIS. And June is engaged to—

JUNE. Nicholas Smith.

TOBY. (*Calls.*) Nick, you've been exposed.

NICK. (*Comes in through panel.*) I've been listening.

JUNE. (*Goes to Nick above sofa.*) See what a family you're marrying into.

NICK. It won't be a boring life.

LOIS. Happy Anniversary you two.

SLOAN. Lois, you are too much.

LOIS. I knew you might solve Cora's murder in the game. That's why we planned the second part with my murder and then poisoning Nick.

TOBY. Maybe you should write and we should publish.

STEPHEN. (*Goes below sofa.*) We rehearsed over a lengthy tax deductible lunch at 21.

LOIS. Weren't they all marvelous? I mean they played one set of people for the first murder and then another set of characters for my death.

SLOAN. We bow in homage to talent.

STEPHEN. I pretended to be a doctor so I could pronounce Lois dead and get Nick to help me carry her upstairs.

NICK. (*Goes to fireplace with June.*) We couldn't let you get too close to Lois.

LOIS. (*Laughs as SHE sits.*) I can only hold my breath for so long.

SLOAN. But the phone calls?

LOIS. That was Virginia from Personnel. I called her when everything was set to go and she was the fake recording.

SLOAN. Wait till I get my hands on her.

TOBY. There's only one thing left to figure out.

LOIS. Which is?

TOBY. (*To BB who has been watching completely absorbed.*) Who are you?

BB. (*Rises and crosses in.*) I am BB Mink. I was invited here for a thousand bucks. I don't understand what is going on but I'm having a wonderful time.

LOIS. She was my surprise for all of you.

NICK. That's dirty, Lois.

LOIS. I wanted to keep you on your toes. I hired her through a theatrical agent.

BB. Yeah and he told me to say I heard about this gig through the personals column and to play along with whatever happened so I have been playing along.

NICK. And we were brilliant to play along with you.

BB. (*Goes C.*) And when this is a TV show I can play Sloan Bigelow.

STEPHEN. How will you ever write this down?

(*The following speeches are all said together.*)

JUNE. (*Goes above sofa.*) I'll have to get an agent, a lawyer, someone to protect my interests ...

STEPHEN. Lois, think of the publicity for the book if it gets written.

NICK. Who will they get to play me? Redford, Baldwin, Pacino?

TOBY. We'll start at the beginning, of course.

SLOAN. They can rent this place for practically nothing.

CORA. This book will make wonderful Christmas gifts.

LOIS. (*Rises and stops them all chattering at once.*) Quiet! Quiet, all of you!

(*THEY quiet down.*)

LOIS. Only two people know how to write this story so let them tell us how it will be. Sloan, Toby, speak.

SLOAN. (*Crosses down below chair.*) We'll start when I came in here.

TOBY. But I was first.

SLOAN. My character is more interesting.

TOBY. I like that.

SLOAN. I'm glad you do because it's true.

LOIS. (*To the others while SLOAN and TOBY continue.*) Let's all go and open some champagne in the kitchen while they settle this. (*Indicates for them to tiptoe out.*)

TOBY. (*During above.*) Do you mean your character the way you're going to write her or your character in real life?

SLOAN. Either one. Everyone knows I am more interesting and amusing than you.

TOBY. And who is everyone? *People* magazine and who else?

SLOAN. Every talk show we've ever been on. They always do more close-ups of me.

TOBY. I didn't have a face-lift.

SLOAN. Are you suggesting I did?

TOBY. When we were audited, the IRS said it was deductible.

(THEY look around and see the OTHERS have gone to the kitchen. THEY smile to each other.)

SLOAN. Now we can sneak out.

TOBY. We'll take Lois' car.

SLOAN. *(As THEY go out the windows.)* And that Jaguar can be our anniversary present.

TOBY. Happy Anniversary, darling.

SLOAN. And the same to you.

(THEY are off and—)

Curtain

PROPERTY PLOT

ACT I, Scene 1:
Preset: phone on shelves, heavy reference books on shelves
Off Up Right:
2 suitcases (TOBY)
Small suitcase, purse with index card (JUNE)
Overnight bag (STEPHEN)
Index card in pocket (STEPHEN)
Purse with index card (CORA)
2 small suitcases (NICK)
Index card in pocket (NICK)
Off Up Left:
3 champagne glasses (TOBY)
Tray with 2 martinis and 2 sodas (TOBY)
Off down Left:
Gift wrapped box with paper in it saying "PLOT" in heavy
    letters and a list of rules. (LOIS)
Shoulder bag (BB)
Shopping bag with bottle of champagne and several books
    by the Bigelows; purse (LOIS)
Distributor cap (LOIS)
Off Right behind panel:
2 canvas director's chairs. (TOBY and NICK)
Page of script paper (TOBY)
Scene 2:
Off left:
Tray with 6 demi-tasse poured, sugar, Sweet 'n Low,
    creamer (TOBY)

ACT II, Scene 1:
Preset: cups, tray cleared, 1 large reference book next to
   one removed
Off Left:
Tray with 4 coffee cups poured, Sweet 'n Low, Creamer
   (TOBY)
2 seltzers (NICK)
Scene 2:
Off Left:
1 Realemon

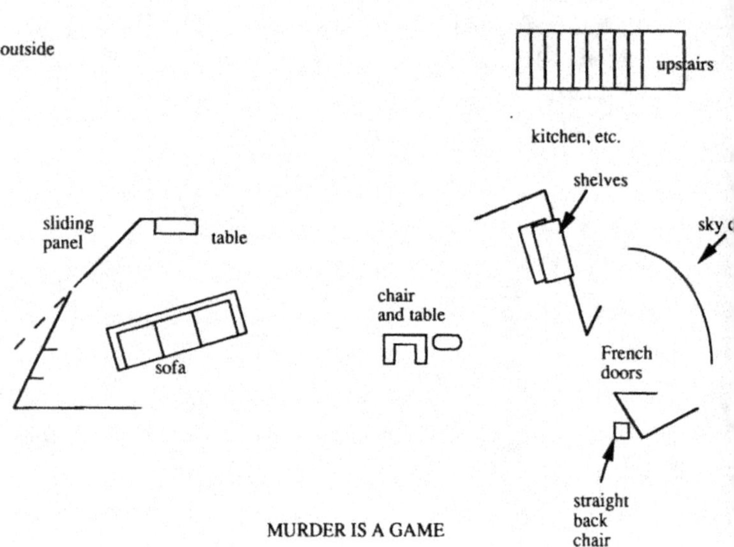

MURDER IS A GAME